The

WARHORSE

The WARHORSE

DON BOLOGNESE

SIMON & SCHUSTER BOOKS FOR YOUNG READERS
New York   London   Toronto   Sydney   Singapore

SIMON & SCHUSTER BOOKS FOR YOUNG READERS
An imprint of Simon & Schuster Children's Publishing Division
1230 Avenue of the Americas, New York, New York 10020

Book design by Paula Winicur
The text for this book is set in Dante.
The illustrations are rendered in colored pencil.
Calligraphy by Don Bolognese

Manufactured in the United States of America
2 4 6 8 10 9 7 5 3 1

Library of Congress Cataloging-in-Publication Data
Bolognese, Don.
The warhorse / Don Bolognese.
p. cm.
Summary: Lorenzo, son of the duke's master armorer, longs to experience battle for himself,
and thrusts himself into conflict when he learns of a planned attack against the duke.
ISBN 0-689-85458-7
[1. Kings, queens, rulers, etc.—Fiction. 2. Armor—Fiction. 3. Horses—Fiction. 4. Artists—
Fiction. 5. Renaissance—Italy—Fiction. 6. Italy—History—1268–1492—Fiction.] I. Title.
PZ7. B63593 War 2003
[Fic]—dc21   2002008199

FIRST
EDITION

To Elaine
for a lifetime of love and inspiration

The WARHORSE

Chapter 1

The rider pulled back on the reins. The white warhorse took several steps back along the river bank, hesitated, then took a few more. "Good boy, Scoppio, good boy. I knew you could do it." The rider, wearing a full suit of armor, leaned forward and patted the neck of the big animal.

"It's almost sunrise, Scoppio; you've had your turn, now it's mine." The dark-haired boy, about fifteen, checked the helmet one more time, then put it on. He pushed the visor up, sat back in his saddle, and waited.

The ground spread out before them into a long narrow strip of turf. At the far end, dark against the early light, stood a tall wooden pole. A long iron spike stuck out from the top. From the spike an object the size of a man swung slowly in the morning breeze. Made of straw stuffed in a rusty suit of armor, the figure gazed blindly at the horse and rider.

The sun rose, catching the straw man by surprise and hurling his shadow across the new grass until it just touched the foot of the horse. "Easy, boy," the rider spoke soothingly, "just a bit longer."

The sun cleared the cathedral dome; its rays swept over the rider's armor, exploding into blinding shafts of light. The boy snapped his visor shut and faced squarely into the rising sun. A hundred paces away his target stood out clearly against the golden sky.

"Perfect! It works!" The rider winced at the echo of his words inside his helmet, but he was pleased. The new visor was just long enough to shield his eyes from direct sunlight. *Now,* he said, this time silently, *let's see if it really works.*

He sat back in the saddle, adjusted the shield on his left forearm, cradled the lance in his right arm, and gathered the reins. At a signal the warhorse leaped forward. His gait picked up quickly. Fifty paces from the target he broke into a full run.

The rider raised his lance until it pointed at the center of the straw man's breastplate. The target, outlined in brilliant sunlight, was still clearly visible through his visor.

Suddenly, without warning, a young boy appeared, waving his arms frantically. Instinctively the rider pulled back on the reins. The charging horse dug his front hooves into the ground, reared, spun around, and let out a loud whinny of protest.

"Easy, boy, easy." The rider, his visor thrown back, spoke sharply, then softly. "Good boy, easy; easy now."

The great animal heaved and pawed at the earth. Breath billowed from his nostrils. Finally, his energy spent, the horse came to a stop.

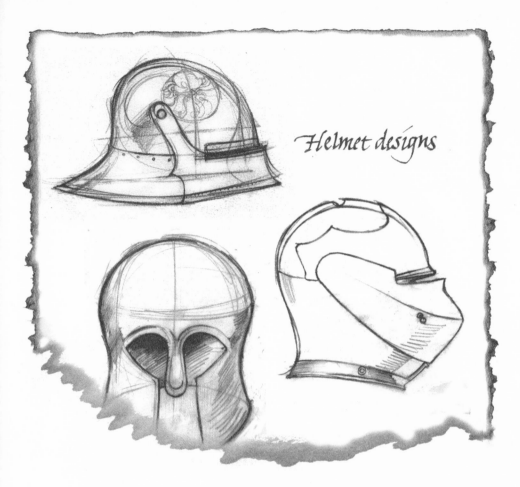

Helmet designs

"Roberto, what are you doing here?" the rider shouted. "Why—"

"The duke—Lorenzo, the duke is on his way to your father's house—look!" The boy pointed to the stone bridge that spanned the river just two hundred paces short of the armory. A party of knights was riding toward the entrance.

"Holy Mother—the duke! My father—the drawings! Roberto, here—" In one motion Lorenzo slid off the saddle, handed the reins to Roberto, and started unbuckling his armor. "Walk him! And make sure he's dry before he drinks."

Lorenzo scrambled up the slope that led to the armory's lower entrance. The hoofbeats of the duke's escort sounded in his ears as he pulled open the heavy wooden door. Sweat streamed down his back as he struggled to free himself of his armor. He looked at his tunic; it was soaked through.

I can't appear this way before the duke, he thought. Above him, the unmistakable sound of men in armor warned him that he had little time to change.

Chapter 2

Master armorer signor Renato Arrighi, maker of the most prized armor in all of Italy, paced back and forth across the marble floor of his studio.

The duke is early, he thought; *a week early. Why? No matter, we are ready: the new hinge works well, the helmet design has been improved and—* He looked through the drawings of armor on his work table. Not finding what he had expected, he searched again.

"Where are Lorenzo's drawings? The duke will ask to see them." Signor Arrighi spoke softly to himself. He was trying to remain calm; trying not to be angry with his son. He looked up; the sound of heavy footsteps echoed through the armory's stone corridor. *Where is that boy? Does he want to disgrace me?*

He was about to call his son's name when the duke appeared in his doorway.

"Signor Arrighi, good morning." The duke's voice

Father wearing the duke's parade armor

suited his countenance. His deep-set, piercing blue eyes and thin, unsmiling lips conveyed the same authority as the somber tone of his greeting.

"Excellency, my lord, it is an honor to have you in my workshop. Please sit here. I have sent for refreshments." Signor Arrighi led the duke to a high-backed upholstered chair.

As the duke sat down signor Arrighi arranged the drawings before him. Signor Arrighi followed his gaze while he studied the drawings. Once again the armorer felt himself captivated by the duke's eyes. The left one was made of glass, and the other good eye looked out from a dark cavity that stretched unbroken across the duke's face. Unlike most men, the duke had no bridge between his eyes. Most of his subjects assumed it was the result of a wound received in battle. But for a few men like the master armorer, who knew the true story, it was stark proof of the duke's ruthless determination.

The refreshments arrived; as a servant began filling the men's goblets, the duke addressed his host.

"Signor Arrighi, I will need the new armor sooner than I had thought. Will you still be able to complete the work?"

"The house of Arrighi has served my lord's family faithfully for five generations. If necessary, my men will work by torchlight. The work will be done; you have my word." The master armorer bowed slightly as he finished his response.

The duke nodded, then turned his attention again to what lay on the table. He picked up a small section of armor and examined it.

"My lord, that is a new hinge I have developed. See

how flexible it is." Signor Arrighi was on familiar ground now and his excitement was obvious.

Holding the hinge in both hands, the duke worked it back and forth. His soldiers, who had gradually crowded around the table, watched intently, trying to imagine how it would function in combat.

"Excellent, master armorer." The duke looked into the faces of his escort. "My knights will have a surprise for our enemies next we meet on the battlefield." A sly smile softened his stern expression. "What else do you have for me today?" The duke searched through the drawings. "The design for my breastplate—is it ready?"

"Yes, my lord, and I believe it has just arrived." Signor Arrighi glared at his son, Lorenzo, who had just appeared in the doorway, red faced and breathless.

The boy, struggling to control his embarrassment, bowed awkwardly to the duke. Fearful of his father's gaze, he fixed his attention on the rolled parchment in his hand. Slowly, almost painfully, he unrolled it and set it in front of the duke.

A small gasp of pleasure escaped the duke's lips; his soldiers, emboldened by their leader's reaction, voiced their praise as well.

Signor Arrighi felt the anger toward his son dissolve, overwhelmed by fatherly pride and admiration for such talent. He tried to catch the boy's eye, but Lorenzo kept his eyes on the drawing.

The duke's hand traced the intricate and delicate

patterns, hovering ever so slightly above the surface so as not to touch the drawing. Finally, almost reluctantly, he turned his attention from the design and looked at the master armorer.

"Signor Arrighi—first the hinge and now—this drawing." The duke paused. "The house of Arrighi continues to add luster to both its reputation and the glory of our city."

The duke stood; his soldiers instantly snapped to attention. The duke started for the door, then stopped and turned toward the boy. Lorenzo, who until now had stubbornly refused to look up, reluctantly and fearfully raised his eyes to face his leader.

The tall, stern man looked directly into the boy's eyes. *He draws like an angel,* the duke thought. *He has the gift, but his will is strong. It needs direction—his father will see to that.*

Signor Arrighi watched the duke studying his son. For a moment he thought the duke would actually speak to the boy, perhaps even praise him personally. But no—the duke nodded to his lieutenant and left as abruptly as he had come.

Chapter 3

"Lorenzo . . ." Signor Arrighi paused while he searched for the right words. "Lorenzo, my son, you know what you mean to me."

The boy, eyes fixed rigidly on his still-muddy boots, could not speak. But his heart ached for the anxiety he had caused his father.

Signor Arrighi walked to the window. Sunlight reflected from the cathedral dome illuminated his face. He stood there awhile, hands folded behind him, thinking, then turned and looked at his son.

"Our Lord God has given us many mysteries, my son. And one of them . . ." Again Lorenzo's father stopped speaking, this time to calm his emotions. He walked over and put his hands on the boy's shoulders. "Son, how does it happen that the same person can cause such pain and so much pleasure at the same time?" And, no longer able to contain his feelings, he pulled his son to him.

Lorenzo, caught in the grip of his father's arms, could only utter a faint, "Forgive me, Father," before tears choked off everything else he was trying to say. He wanted to apologize for his selfishness, for not being there when the duke arrived—a minute later and he would have brought great shame to his father—but he could not say the words.

With one arm still around the boy's shoulder, signor Arrighi turned toward the window that looked out over the city. "Lorenzo, look at this beautiful city. For almost two hundred years, the house of Arrighi has been its sword and its shield. That is a great responsibility—and someday it will be all yours to bear."

"Father, I know that. I know I am foolish and thoughtless—especially when it comes to my horse. I . . . I can't seem to help myself—but I will try harder. I promise."

His father smiled a sad smile. "You have a good heart, my son. Your mother, God rest her soul, always said that of you. But now you are going to need courage as well."

Something in his father's voice made Lorenzo fearful. "I don't understand, Father."

Signor Arrighi walked slowly to the chair that only minutes earlier had held the duke. "The duke's visit this morning was unexpected; his next visit was not due for another week. I think I know the reason—the duke fears for our city. He believes it is in great danger, perhaps greater than at any time in its history. He suspects war is near."

Lorenzo grew more concerned. "Why, Father? How

could that be? The duke is a great warrior—his enemies fear and respect him."

"As do our allies. Their loyalty to us has kept our ancient enemy, Florence, at bay." Lorenzo's father stopped, as if not wanting to continue, but he went on. "There are rumors that one of our oldest allies has been bought off by the Florentines, and that they've hired a mercenary army from Germany. . . ."

"I have heard of the German knights, Father. Massimo has fought against them and . . ."

"So, is that who is telling you all these war stories? Is he the one filling your head with the glories of war? Is that why you spend so much time training to be a knight on that warhorse of yours?" Suddenly signor Arrighi's fear for the safety of his city turned to fear for his son's future. "Your training in arms is to be used only for our work here in the armory; I will never allow you to go to war. Never!"

Lorenzo felt as if he had been kicked in the stomach; he hadn't meant to excite his father or threaten the bond between his father and Massimo. Not only was Massimo his father's best armorer, he was his father's oldest friend. "It is not Massimo's fault, Father. He was showing me some foreign armor, made in Germany. I asked him how he had gotten it, and I kept asking for more and more details. Please, Father, don't blame him—he knows how you feel about my being a knight."

The elder Arrighi looked at his son; his expression softened. "I know, Lorenzo, I know. Massimo has seen enough blood spilled to wash away any feelings of glory. I know he wishes that our armor were only ceremonial, just made for parades and pageants." Lorenzo's father turned again toward the window. "But, my son, I'm afraid the duke needs our armor because a war is coming, and coming sooner than any of us would like."

Chapter 4

Billows of smoke and blasts of fiery heat engulfed Lorenzo as he entered the armory. The armorers at their anvils, their sweat-soaked bodies glistening in the light of the blazing forges, looked like tortured souls writhing in the fires of hell. The sounds of the armory were brutal: hammers pounding incessantly, the loud hissing as white-hot iron slabs plunged into vats of cold water, the groans of men pushed beyond endurance, the shouting and cursing when apprentices failed to follow commands. *Yes,* Lorenzo thought, reminded of a panel in an altarpiece he had just seen. *It is a living painting of hell.*

The leader of the armory workers was Massimo, the strongest man Lorenzo had ever known. This morning, as usual, he worked relentlessly, hammering, flattening, and shaping a huge slab of steel into a breastplate for the duke's warhorse. Not many men had the strength and ability to fashion such large pieces into armor. It was demanding and exhausting work, and no one in the house of Arrighi did it better.

Lorenzo had been his apprentice. He had learned everything he knew about metalworking from Massimo. And now he needed all those skills. With war a real possibility, every piece of armor could be the difference between

Massimo

Light armor – a brigandine over mail

victory and defeat. And he had been given a special honor—the making of a new helmet for the duke himself.

Lorenzo had worked late into the previous night. He'd slept a few hours, then, before sunrise, had gone to pray. He had implored the Holy Mother to protect their city; and to make him a better, more dutiful son.

He stood in front of his forge; the blue flames darting above red-hot coals told him the fire was ready. It was time to get back to work.

Carefully, using long tongs, Lorenzo turned the helmet in the coals until it glowed; in minutes it was ready for the anvil. The pounding made sparks fly, most of them bouncing harmlessly off his leather apron. Some dove, hissing, into the water bucket; a few embers seared his bare forearms. But nothing could slow his progress.

As the day wore on, fatigue began to take its toll. Two apprentices had collapsed and one ironworker had broken his left hand. But the work continued; even signor Arrighi put on his leather apron to work personally on the duke's new armor.

Just before sundown the frenzy in the workshop reached a level Lorenzo had never seen; it was as if everyone knew that time was slipping away. Or maybe it was all the rumors flooding the city—the Florentines gathering their forces; German mercenaries seen marching into Italy; the duke's oldest ally marrying his daughter to a Florentine noble. Were these stories true? No one knew, but the fear in the city grew stronger.

So intent was Lorenzo on finishing the duke's helmet, he didn't notice the sudden silence in the workshop. Not until his assistant touched his arm did he lower his hammer and look up.

There, framed in the arched doorway, surrounded by his escort, was the duke. He was about to speak.

Chapter 5

The duke's gaze was intense. Every man and boy felt the duke was looking straight into his soul.

Signor Arrighi, recovering from his surprise at this second unexpected visit, began to speak, but the duke raised his hand; he had something to tell them.

"I have come here," the duke began, "to see for myself what others have told me." He looked directly at signor Arrighi. "The city and I have much to thank you for. Our enemies would not be comforted by what I see here today. And soon, on the field of battle, they will *feel* the results of your labor."

At that, the men, with one voice, shouted their approval.

Signor Arrighi was embarrassed by his men's response. Not so, the duke; he nodded slowly, smiling. Finally, with another glance in the direction of the master armorer, the duke turned and, followed by his escort, left.

Everyone in the workshop began to talk at once. Lorenzo was excited, but puzzled by what had just happened. Public expressions of gratitude by the duke were almost unheard of. Absolute loyalty and total sacrifice from his subjects were his due; he expected nothing less.

Lorenzo was on his way to ask Massimo his opinion when a servant of the duke came into the room. Lorenzo saw the man speak briefly to his father and leave, then saw his father signal the apprentices to move some tables. They had barely finished when the duke's servant returned, this time leading a train of servants carrying baskets of delicacies from the duke's kitchen, followed by two more servants struggling with huge flagons of wine.

Another shout went up from the men, but this time it was one of surprise and pleasure at the sight of such a feast.

Signor Arrighi signaled for silence. "The duke has truly honored us today. . . ." He hesitated, not quite over his own surprise. "His Excellency has noted the sacrifices you are making. His visit, the refreshments, the wine from his own cellars—these would be more than enough proof that he values our work." The master armorer picked up a small leather sack left by the duke's servant and held it up for all the men to see. "But our duke wanted the entire city to know the debt it owes to the workers of the Arrighi armory." Every man's attention was riveted on the leather sack held aloft by their master. Signor Arrighi turned toward Massimo. "He has awarded each master ironworker three gold ducats, and each apprentice—" The head of the house of Arrighi never got to finish what he was saying; the shout that followed drowned out all further attempts at speech.

Lorenzo was shouting too. He had always looked up to the duke, always loved his city, but now he would gladly give his life for them.

Lorenzo looked for Massimo; everyone was milling around, talking, eating, toasting each other and their good fortune. The strain of the past weeks, the brutal hours, the bruised and tortured muscles—all of it seemed to vanish in the glow of the duke's generosity.

"Massimo, Massimo . . ." Lorenzo tried to get the shop master's attention; it was Massimo's skill that set the standards, his will that motivated every worker. Lorenzo wanted to congratulate him, to share this rare moment with him. "Massimo," the boy shouted over the din, finally getting his attention.

Massimo looked at Lorenzo, but he wasn't smiling. His eyes were distant. They seemed to be looking somewhere beyond Lorenzo, beyond the crowd of happy men, beyond the very moment itself.

Suddenly, Lorenzo no longer felt like celebrating. All the good feelings drained out of him. *What,* he asked himself, *is Massimo thinking?*

Chapter 6

Lorenzo pushed through the noisy crowd to Massimo's side.

Massimo turned to the boy, his expression unchanged. "Lorenzo, you must be very proud. The duke has honored the house of Arrighi . . ."

"But, Massimo, you weren't cheering; aren't you proud?" Lorenzo interrupted his mentor. He looked deep into Massimo's eyes searching for an answer.

Massimo put his arm on the boy's shoulder and led him to a quiet corner of the workshop.

"Lorenzo, sit down. I have to tell you a story." Massimo remained standing by a window that overlooked the city. The familiar sounds of their city drifted through the open window.

"You are my godson; your father is my oldest friend. When I lost my wife and children to the terrible sickness that swept through our city twenty years ago, your father's friendship was the only reason I did not go mad. He convinced me to enlist in the duke's service. It was not easy, but it saved my life.

"I've told you a few stories from that time. But there is one I have not repeated. . . ." The older man stopped and looked at the scene below. Rays from the late afternoon sun had turned the river into a ribbon of silver. *Like a sash on the gown of a beautiful woman,* thought Massimo, and a long forgotten vision of his young wife flashed before him. Quickly he grabbed the back of a chair to steady himself; the many years had not diminished his grief—or his longing.

"Are you all right, Massimo?" Lorenzo held out a hand to his godfather. "Can I get you something, some water?"

"No, no . . . I'll be all right, but it's very dangerous to dig up memories." Massimo smiled. "They're like mushrooms after a heavy rain—they pop up all over the place, both good and bad."

Lorenzo smiled at the joke Massimo had made on himself. The shop master was always being teased about his passion for wild mushrooms. He could hear his father scolding his friend—"Massimo, if you insist on serving me those mushrooms, I will never eat at your house again." Then, with great ceremony, Massimo would put a huge forkful into his own mouth, chew it well, and, with an elaborate gesture of outspread arms, announce: "See, signor Renato Arrighi. I, your old friend and comrade, Massimo, still live. So—eat!" Lorenzo had seen this little drama many times, a sign of the love and trust shared by the two men.

Massimo's smile began to fade. "This story, Lorenzo, may help explain what I was feeling before.

"I fought alongside the duke for five years; they were hard times. Our enemies were determined to destroy us. But the duke's courage and mastery of war stood in their way. He was younger then, stronger and quicker. In the saddle or on his feet, he was fearless. Once I saw him cleave a man in half—armor and all." Massimo turned his head to one side as if trying to hide from the bloody image.

"It was in that battle that the incident happened.

"The fighting was over; we had won. The dead and wounded were lying all about, some crying out for help. The duke raised his visor to congratulate us, his personal guards. We were relieved and exhausted. At one point we had been surrounded and outnumbered; we were glad to be alive.

"Suddenly one of the enemy wounded got up, screamed something in German, and threw his dagger at the duke. One of my comrades threw his battle-ax at the man, severing his head, but it was already too late."

The power of the old soldier's story transfixed the boy. He could see it clearly: the battlefield, the man, the dagger, the ax flying through the air, blood spurting from a headless body. *But what does he mean, "too late"?*

Massimo continued, "We were so intent on the soldier, we forgot about the dagger. When we turned back to the duke, his hand was to his face, blood flowing through his fingers. I rushed to him, to keep him from falling. I saw the dagger at his feet. When I looked up, he had taken his hand from his face, and . . ."

Lorenzo looked into Massimo's face. He could see the horror Massimo was feeling.

"I'm sorry, my boy, it's another of those memories better left buried." Massimo took a long look out the window, then turned and continued, "In his hand was his eye . . . it was horrible. We carried the duke to his tent. He never made a sound, never cried out. Finally, when we had stopped the bleeding, he sent for his surgeon. I remember wondering at the time why he sent for the doctor *after* we had tended his wound.

"When the surgeon arrived, he immediately tried to dress the wound. The duke brushed him aside and told him to get his small hammer and bone chisel. Then the duke had us strap his legs and arms to his cot. And he ordered me to hold his head as tight as possible.

"Finally he told the surgeon he wanted the bridge of his nose removed. At first the doctor didn't understand, so the duke had me untie one of his arms so he could point to the part he wanted removed.

"The frightened surgeon was afraid the duke had gone mad. But the duke pulled the doctor close to him and spoke very softly. That convinced him, because he took a piece of charcoal from the fire and drew a small semicircle on the duke's nose. He gave the duke a drink of very strong brandy. While we waited for the brandy to take effect the surgeon bandaged the duke's good eye to protect it from

His Excellency — the duke

bone splinters, and we made sure the irons for sealing the wound were red-hot.

"Finally the duke signaled he was ready. He had me put a thick leather belt in his mouth, clenched his teeth and nodded to the surgeon." Massimo was holding his head; sweat had broken out on his forehead, but he went on. "A few minutes later—a lot more blood—and it was over."

Lorenzo stood up. For more than a minute he was silent. "I always thought it was a war wound." His voice was little more than a whisper. "I never imagined it was self-inflicted. But why?"

"Think, Lorenzo—you're a good swordsman. The duke lost his left eye—his undefended side." Massimo pretended he had a sword in his right hand.

"Of course," Lorenzo reasoned aloud. "He needed a line of sight to his left. The bridge of his nose blocked the view from his good eye." The boy nodded slowly, trying to put himself in the duke's place. "Now I understand why you call the duke fearless and determined . . . and ruthless. But how does the story explain your feelings about his visit this afternoon?"

The old soldier pulled a steel gauntlet onto his hand and picked a pear from one of the duke's baskets. As Lorenzo watched, Massimo crushed the pear in his steel fist. Juice ran down his arm, pulp squirted out from between the metal fingers, and when Massimo opened his fist only a few pits remained.

"That's what the duke did to all his enemies—and to any ally who betrayed him. The duke I fought beside never gave gifts or compliments. Fear of him was enough. But he is older now, and tired. He has no son to share the burden of leadership, and I believe he's finally had a visit from a stranger he never expected—fear. I think his enemies, and his allies, know this."

Massimo took the boy by the arm and walked toward the forges. "And I am very sure of one thing, Lorenzo: The duke needs us—now more than ever."

Chapter 7

For days Lorenzo could not get Massimo's story out of his mind. *What if Massimo is right?* he asked himself. *What if the duke has lost the respect of his allies and they desert him—and join forces with the Florentines? Will there be war?*

These doubts and fears exhausted him; even sleep gave no relief. His dreams were filled with strange and frightening images—knights covered with spikes, carrying lances of fire, all charging straight at him. In the nightmares he was always alone, on his horse, outside the city, with no armor, no weapons, and no escape. He would wake up covered in sweat, then hurry back to his work—*that* was his escape.

"Lorenzo, my boy." Massimo had just arrived in the armory. The eastern sky was brightening, but some stars were still visible. "You are at work so early—can't you sleep?"

The boy kept hammering at the armor on his anvil. He seemed not to hear his godfather.

"Lorenzo." The older man called again, then walked

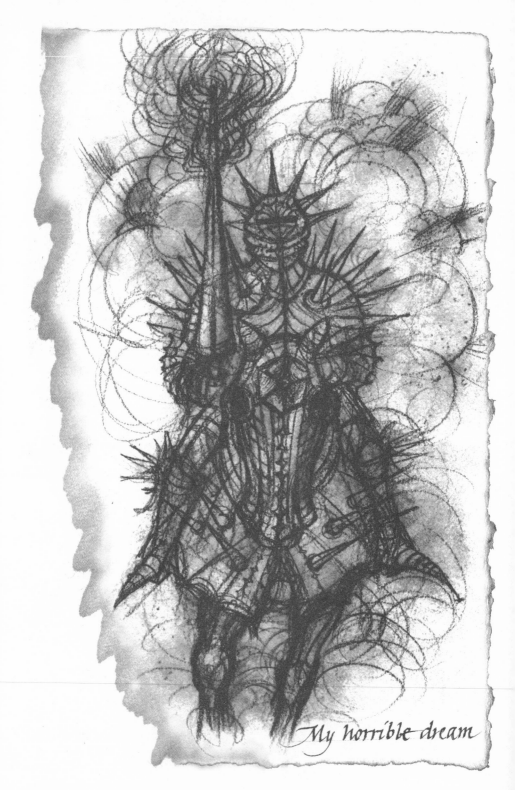

My horrible dream

over to the boy. "Are you all right? Your father and I are concerned. You're not eating, not talking—you seem to be miles away. What is wrong?"

The boy started to deny anything was wrong, but Massimo interrupted him. "Something is bothering you and I can guess what it is: the story about the duke. Am I right?"

The boy's silence confirmed Massimo's guess. He put a hand on his godson's shoulder. "Listen to me, Lorenzo. It's true, these are dangerous times. A city like ours is a tempting prize to an ambitious count with dreams of glory. We can expect intrigue, treachery, even armed attacks. But I promise you, we will not be an easy prize." Massimo started walking toward his forge, then turned and said with a smile, "Remember, I'm just an old soldier whose brains have been rattled by too many blows on the helmet—I could be all wrong about the duke." The shop master went back to his forge and told his assistant to build up the fire. He was ready for another day of hard work.

A smile appeared on Lorenzo's face—it was the first one in days. *Massimo is a good man,* he thought. *I shouldn't have worried him and my father; they have enough problems.* The boy picked up his hammer and continued what he'd been doing.

About midmorning, an apprentice walking past a window began shouting, "Quickly, come look at this!"

Massimo and Lorenzo put aside their tools and went to look.

A cluster of pennants emblazoned with the duke's coat of arms fluttered just above the food stalls that lined the road leading to the city's south gate. The duke was making a ceremonial visit outside the city. A crowd had already gathered alongside the arched gates opening onto the road that ran south through the duke's vast farmlands. They were cheering and waving maroon and gold pennants.

Moments later the entire troop came into Lorenzo's view. The boy was thrilled by the column of knights dressed in full parade armor. The captain of the guard led the column, then more knights. Behind them rode the duke, followed by more knights and soldiers, each one carrying a lance with a pennant.

After watching for a minute, Massimo tapped Lorenzo's shoulder.

"Do you see anything unusual?"

Lorenzo looked puzzled. He searched the scene below for some clue to Massimo's question. Suddenly he saw it. He nodded, then turned from the window and walked back to his forge.

Massimo followed and sat down on a bench facing the boy.

"Well, what was it?" The old soldier's face did not betray his own thoughts and feelings.

"The duke's breastplate—it was his father's. I have never seen him wear it before," Lorenzo answered.

Massimo nodded in agreement. "I first saw that suit of ceremonial armor when I was a child. The duke was a very young man then, only a little older than you are now. His father was taking him on his first diplomatic visit to a new ally. That day the old duke wore the armor that his son is wearing today. Did you know that the embossed breastplate with gold inlay was made by your father?"

"I know. That was the first piece of armor father had me study; he is very proud of it." The young armorer paused, then looked into the eyes of his friend and mentor. "So, Massimo, the rumor about one of our allies *is* true," Lorenzo said.

"Yes," Massimo agreed. "The duke hopes that wearing his father's old armor will remind this old ally of his oath of loyalty—and the painful consequences of betrayal."

"Do you think he'll succeed?" Lorenzo asked. "The truth, Massimo—I have to know."

The old soldier got up and walked over to his forge. He signaled his apprentice to work the bellows. "Hurry, Niccolo, the fire is going down; work the bellows—harder." Massimo's tone was impatient; he seemed irritable. He avoided answering Lorenzo.

After a moment or two Lorenzo resumed his work too.

In the middle of shaping a piece of armor, Massimo stopped and went to Lorenzo's side.

"In a week the threat of flooding from the spring rains will be past." He spoke slowly, and softly, as if dreading the sound of his own words, "The ground will harden—enough to support columns of armored knights. Then, God save our city, the horrors of war will be upon us."

Chapter 8

Lorenzo was already awake when the first rays of sunlight brightened the woven tapestry that hung on the wall behind his bed.

He had not slept well; the memory of the previous day's events refused to go away, especially Massimo's words. The images of the horrors of war sent chills through him.

That feeling was in sharp contrast to the warm day the sunrise seemed to promise. The young armorer got up and dressed. He had decided to do something other than worry.

The first thing is to deliver the armor that is ready, he thought. *Then if anything happens, the duke will at least have that much on hand. It will also give me a chance to exercise Scoppio; he's not been ridden lately.* Lorenzo ran to the kitchen, grabbed a slice of goat cheese, stuffed it into a chunk of freshly baked bread, and hurried to the shop.

"Wake up, Roberto!" The young Arrighi threw the covers off the apprentice, who during the recent hectic period had taken to sleeping in the workshop. "We have work to do! Get Niccolo and load the wagon with all the armor that is ready. I'll go and get the horses. And tell Massimo what we're doing; he'll want to know."

Lorenzo quickly went to the stables underneath the workshop. He gathered the harnesses and began hitching a team of horses to the heavily built wagon they used to transport the armor.

Niccolo and Roberto began the exhausting job of lowering the armor into the wagon through a trapdoor built into the shop floor. Lorenzo inspected each piece, then covered it in burlap so it would not be scratched during the trip. Lorenzo always thought it funny that his father worried that everything look perfect—after all, armor was made to suffer abuse—but Lorenzo respected his father and knew this was only one more example of the pride he had in his work.

"Lorenzo, we are finished. There are a few more pieces, but that load is almost too heavy now." Roberto looked through the trapdoor, waiting for a reply.

"You're right, Roberto; come down. Take the load to the palace. Niccolo, stay here; Massimo will need you. Have you seen him this morning?"

"No, but I was told he did not go home. He spent the night in the tower." Niccolo sounded surprised at his master's decision.

So, Massimo is as worried as I am. What is he looking for up there? Lorenzo wondered as he fought to keep focused on the job at hand. He grabbed the bridle of one of the horses and led the team to the courtyard as Roberto scrambled down the stairs.

The apprentice climbed onto the wagon, took the reins, and snapped them lightly. The horses strained at the harness, then slowly pulled the wagon up a slight incline and onto the main road.

"I'll catch up with you in a minute," Lorenzo called out as he attempted to saddle Scoppio. The huge warhorse was prancing about, his energy bursting to get out. He had been stabled for too long. "Easy, Scoppio, easy. I'm as eager as you are to get going." The boy struggled to tighten the cinch and steady the horse at the same time.

Finally he succeeded and pulled himself into the saddle; he never failed to be thrilled by the sense of power he felt astride his warhorse. He eased the impatient animal out into the courtyard and turned toward the road.

"Lorenzo, Lorenzo!" The boy turned in his saddle; Massimo was calling to him from the stairs. With one hand he held onto the rail; with the other he grasped his right thigh.

"What is it, Massimo?"

"Lorenzo, you must tell them at the palace . . ." The older man lurched across the stable toward Lorenzo, grasping at the horse's reins to steady himself. He was near fainting from the pain in his bad leg. "From the tower—" Massimo gasped. "I've seen them from the tower . . ." Massimo started to fall.

Lorenzo jumped from the saddle and caught the older man in his arms. "Who have you seen?" he cried.

Massimo could barely speak, the pain was so intense. "German mercenaries—under Florentine banners—heading this way. I think they plan to cut off the duke's return."

"But how did they know—" Lorenzo began.

Massimo struggled to his feet. "It doesn't matter. But you must warn the palace. They need to send a relief column to the duke—now!"

Lorenzo mounted his horse. "Send Niccolo to the palace. I'm going to warn the duke. His camp is five miles away and every minute counts."

Weapons for the army

"You cannot go!" Massimo held fast to the horse's bridle. "If anything happens to you, your father . . ."

"Let go, Massimo." The boy pulled back on the reins, jerking the horse's head up and out of Massimo's grasp.

Horse and rider lunged out of the courtyard and down the hillside to the riverbank. Lorenzo had one goal—to warn the duke. If swimming the river saved time, that's what he'd do. He paused only a second at the river's edge; the water was muddy and cold from the spring thaw, and the current was strong, but not for his horse. With a yell, he and Scoppio plunged into the river.

Chapter 9

The big horse swam strongly across the current. Lorenzo gambled that crossing the river instead of using the bridge would save time.

Halfway across, the boy looked to his right. About five hundred paces downstream the river passed under the city wall through an arched tunnel. A horse and rider would go through it easily. Lorenzo reasoned he would reach the road sooner by using the underpass. He tugged on the right rein and headed his horse downstream.

Swimming with the current was easier for Scoppio; they were moving quickly toward the underpass. Fifty paces from its near side, Lorenzo saw dark shapes silhouetted against the light; iron bars suspended from the tunnel's ceiling. He knew their purpose instantly—to keep enemy boats from entering the city.

Lorenzo anxiously guessed at the space between the bars; just enough for a horse, but not with a rider. He cursed himself for his cleverness; he should have settled for the gate. But it was too late for regrets, no time to turn for shore. He prayed there was enough space. He slipped his feet from the stirrups and stretched out along the horse's back.

Scoppio was swimming toward the light. Ten paces to go—five—his head went through—good. Suddenly they were caught. Scoppio pawed stubbornly at the water.

Lorenzo knew Scoppio would drown if he didn't keep moving. The boy rolled off the horse and into the water. The silt in the river blinded him—he could feel the horse thrashing wildly. Lorenzo jammed his hand along its heaving flanks and found the problem, a stirrup caught on a bar. He pulled his dagger and quickly cut the leather strap. Scoppio lurched forward, his right rear leg lashing out. It caught Lorenzo on the shoulder and sent him deeper into the water.

Lorenzo, his lungs bursting, frantically swam to the surface. Scoppio had had enough water, and he headed for the closest bank.

Thank God, Lorenzo prayed silently as he watched his horse clamber up the muddy slope and onto solid ground. He followed Scoppio out of the water, stumbling up the slippery bank and falling full length onto the warm grass.

The warhorse came and stood over his master and, as if to remind him of his mission, pawed the ground.

"Sorry, boy—that was too close." Lorenzo got to his feet, tried once to rub the river mud off his saddle with his tunic, then gave up. "You're right, boy. We have no time to lose." He threw the water-soaked saddle and his wet tunic to the ground. "Now, let's see how fast you can run without that weight."

Lorenzo grabbed a handful of mane and pulled himself onto the horse. He dug his heels sharply into its flanks and held on tight. The big animal charged down the road to the duke's camp.

Chapter 10

The horse and rider raced south. The duke's life was at stake.

German mercenaries—God help us! Lorenzo prayed that he would reach the duke before the Florentines attacked. "Go, Scoppio, go!" Lorenzo urged on his charger, grateful for the horse's speed. Free of the heavy saddle, the horse flew down the road. Peddlers and travelers scrambled out of their way, shouting curses at them as they passed, but the rider didn't care; the Florentines were his only concern. He looked for anything—a flash of sunlight off a shield, a helmet—anything that would reveal the presence of the enemy.

In another mile the road veered away from the river, went up a slight incline and crossed a clearing that opened onto a view of the valley. Lorenzo reined in his horse. He looked for signs of the enemy.

He saw nothing, but he knew better. They could be

hiding anywhere, waiting for just the right moment to spring their ambush.

He kept riding. Lorenzo passed a line of cypress trees, left the road and headed across a sunny meadow. Bright with the first blooms of spring, it was a stark contrast to the dark thoughts of war that filled the boy's head.

He crossed the meadow and entered a grove of olive trees. Beyond them, a half mile away, ruins of an ancient Roman temple shimmered in the sunlight. Lorenzo knew it was one of the duke's favorite places. He pointed Scoppio in that direction, and moments later he caught sight of maroon and gold pennants waving above a large tent, but there was no sign of the duke's ally. As he was wondering why, two sentries rode out from behind a growth of pine trees and signaled him to halt.

Barely slowing his pace he called out to them, "I come with a warning for the duke!"

One of the soldiers recognized him and shouted back, "Lorenzo Arrighi, what is it, why are you here?"

"No time—must see the duke—the Florentines are coming!"

Mention of the hated enemy sent all three on a furious sprint to the duke's tent. The duke was waiting for them, their shouts having already alerted the entire camp.

Lorenzo dismounted at a run. The boy's appearance meant trouble and the duke wasted no time in getting at the reason.

"What is it, Lorenzo; is there trouble at the palace?"

"No, my lord." Lorenzo, nearly breathless from excitement, told the duke what Massimo had seen.

"The cowardly dogs!" The duke exploded. Then, fearful of alarming his men, he fought to contain his anger. He turned aside and growled a string of orders to his aides.

The duke's escort, all experienced fighting men, had sensed trouble. In minutes they had put on their weapons and saddled their mounts.

Lorenzo was back on Scoppio and moving toward the rear of the column when one of the duke's aides signaled to him.

"Signor Arrighi, His Excellency, the duke, wishes you to ride beside him. Follow me."

The boy was astonished, and honored, not only by the request, but by the way the aide had addressed him: "signor Arrighi."

"Lorenzo," the duke began, his expression alert, watching as the captain of the guard deployed the men according to his orders, "was the palace warned?"

"Yes, my lord, and a relief column is surely on its way at this very moment." Only when he had finished speaking did Lorenzo realize how boldly he had spoken to the duke.

The duke had noticed as well, but not wanting to embarrass the boy further, he continued, "You will ride at my side until we are safely within the city. I would not want your father distressed by having anything happen to you."

That seemed to end their conversation. The column had gotten under way quickly, and soon it had reached the meadow. But Lorenzo was nervous; they were not moving fast enough. Their full parade armor was slowing them down, especially the scouts. He suspected that the enemy would be lightly armored, and use speed and surprise as weapons. If the duke hoped to avoid capture, or worse, he would have to be ready for the Florentines; he could not survive an ambush. Lorenzo guessed the duke knew this already and was searching for a solution.

It was midday. The sun was high in the sky and the air was getting hot. Both men and horses were beginning to tire. Lorenzo was glad to be free of his tunic and saddle; Scoppio still felt fresh and strong. He and his horse were being wasted back with the duke. They should be up front with the scouts.

"Pardon me, Your Excellency, may I speak about a concern I have," Lorenzo began, then turned red with shame for having spoken without permission.

The duke looked at the boy curiously, as if seeing him for the first time. *Who is this boy?* he wondered. *He is respectful, even afraid of me, yet he has the courage to speak and, I suspect, even offer me advice.*

"Continue, Lorenzo, you may speak. What are your concerns?"

Chapter 11

Lorenzo spoke to the duke quickly, before his courage failed. When he had finished, his face was flushed with excitement.

The duke had only one problem: his concern for the boy's safety. He knew the boy was right, that they needed as much warning as possible if they were going to hold off a superior force until help came. Scoppio was a magnificent animal, his rider sharp-witted and observant. If the enemy *was* planning an ambush, he would see it. But the thought of signor Arrighi's grief, should anything happen to the boy, was painful and made him hesitate.

One of his soldiers rode up. "Your Excellency, one of our scouts—"

"Has he seen the enemy?" the duke interrupted his lieutenant.

"No, sire, one of the horses has gone lame. The scout needs a new mount. The captain thought the boy's horse would be a good replacement." The lieutenant shot a quick glance at Lorenzo.

The duke looked straight ahead, his gaze fixed on the horizon. "The captain is right." Out of the corner of his good eye the duke saw Lorenzo's face go completely pale. "But the boy stays on the horse. These are my orders. The boy is not to go more than a half mile beyond our nearest rider. If he sights any sign of the enemy he should return immediately. If he meets the relief force he should tell them of our position, then return to the city." The duke paused. "If we are forced to fight, I want to be positioned on the rise about three miles north of here, at the clearing. I don't want the cowards hiding in the trees, shooting their cross-bows at us. Tell the captain that is our first objective. Go!"

"Yes, sire!" The lieutenant signaled to Lorenzo and the pair rode quickly to the head of the troop. The captain was waiting.

Lorenzo watched and waited as the lieutenant repeated the duke's words. The captain had removed his helmet. His bald skull was covered with sweat. He listened to the lieutenant without expression, then turned to Lorenzo.

"You've heard the duke's orders?" He spoke while refastening his helmet.

"Yes, sir," the boy answered.

"Good, and remember, the duke is never disobeyed." He snapped his visor shut and rode off.

Lorenzo looked at the lieutenant, nodded slightly, dug his heels into Scoppio and took off at a run. He could scarcely believe what he was—a point scout for the duke, searching for the enemy. He knew the Florentines would strike, maybe in an ambush. They'd try to kill or capture the duke, maybe hold him for ransom. And there would be fighting, and killing. *Mother of God, protect me, save our city,* he prayed to the Virgin, and to the soul of his own mother, who had died when he was only a boy.

Halfway across the meadow, a wave of fear swept over him; it fell on his shoulders like cold wet snow, then sank to the pit of his stomach and hardened into a knot that twisted and turned with every pounding hoofbeat. Finally his body couldn't take it anymore. Holding on to Scoppio's mane, he leaned out as far as he could, and threw up.

Feelings of relief and shame brought him to tears. He angrily brushed them away; but he couldn't as easily get rid of the doubts that flooded his heart. *I don't have enough courage to be a soldier,* he thought. *But,* he scolded himself, *don't worry about that now.*

Scoppio jumped over a shallow ditch; they had reached the road. Somewhere out there, waiting for the duke, was the enemy.

Chapter 12

Lorenzo looked everywhere for signs of an ambush. Every stand of trees and each turn in the road was suspect.

As he cantered past a small thicket he remembered that it concealed an ancient shrine; a perfect hiding place for anyone watching the road.

He hadn't gone another fifty paces when four mounted soldiers suddenly appeared from the direction of the ruin. One, apparently the leader, rode directly into Lorenzo's path.

"Hold, boy, a word with you," he called out.

His accent, Lorenzo realized, was Florentine. His manners were those of a superior addressing a simple peasant.

"My men and I," the soldier continued, "are on our way to the estate of Count Negroli. Is this the right road?"

This soldier must think me a stupid stable hand who has never left the farm, Lorenzo thought. *Count Negroli is an ally of the duke and lives north, not south of here. He is after something, so I will play his game.*

Roman shrine on the south road

"Forgive me, sire, I know nothing of that count," Lorenzo answered humbly. "I am only delivering my master's horse to his brother in the city. My master lost a wager and cannot bear to deliver this magnificent animal himself."

The soldier seemed amused by Lorenzo's story. The others, the boy noticed, did not react. Then it came to him: *They didn't understand me because they are foreigners.*

The soldier moved closer to Scoppio; he ran his hand over the warhorse's flank. "A fine animal," he said. Scoppio stamped impatiently.

The soldier continued, "Tell me, boy, have you passed

any men on the way? Some of the count's guard may be out looking for us. We are long overdue."

As Lorenzo considered his reply he noticed one of the foreign soldiers—a bareheaded, blond youth, not much older than he—move toward Scoppio. The foreigner could not take his eyes off the horse; Lorenzo saw the leader look at him sharply.

"I have only passed some peddlers," Lorenzo responded finally, "and . . . oh, yes, a shepherd driving his flock to market."

The soldier looked past the boy to the road behind him; a small dust cloud hovered above the distant trees.

The soldier nodded in the direction of the city. "On your way!"

Lorenzo saluted the soldier respectfully and urged his horse forward, but not too quickly; he didn't want to arouse any suspicions. And he dared not look back.

About two hundred paces up the road he came to a halt, dismounted and tied Scoppio to a tree. He undid his pants as if to relieve himself, then glanced back down the road to see if he was being watched.

They *were* watching. But in a minute or two they lost interest, turned and left the road. *Hopefully,* Lorenzo thought, *to go and make their own report.*

"Thank you, Lord!" the boy prayed aloud as he led his horse into the cover of the woods and turned south. "We can't get back on the road, boy, not yet." Talking to his horse relieved some of his fear, helped him think more clearly.

He quickened his pace; soon he was even with the old shrine. "A little farther, Scoppio, and I think we can risk getting on the road." The horse snorted and chewed on his bit; he was eager to run.

Finally they passed the ruins. Lorenzo remounted and eased the horse onto the road. The way looked clear. It was time to report to the duke.

"Go, Scoppio! Run—to the duke!" The boy snapped the reins, held on tightly, and let his horse run free.

Chapter 13

"Massimo, Lorenzo!" Signor Arrighi rushed into the armory. "Lorenzo, Massimo—where are those two? Niccolo, come here!" The master armorer gestured to Massimo's assistant.

"Yes, sire?" The apprentice ran into the workshop.

"Where are Lorenzo and Massimo? I'm gone for two days, and when I return, everything is confused. Even the duke's palace—when I passed, it was in a state of chaos. What is happening?"

"I'm sorry, sire—" the young apprentice was frightened by signor Arrighi's anger "—the palace is sending a relief force to rescue the duke."

The master armorer collapsed onto a bench. "What . . . ," he began weakly.

Quickly Niccolo recounted the morning's events, including Lorenzo's decision to warn the duke personally.

Signor Arrighi sat hunched over, his head in his hands, his

world upside down. "And Massimo?" he asked. "Where is he?"

Niccolo fought back tears as he told of the old soldier's determination to go to the duke's palace. "He was in great pain, sire, but he made me help him onto his horse . . . I couldn't keep him here."

"And Lorenzo? How long has he been gone?"

"Over . . . over an hour, sire." The boy seemed reluctant to answer.

"Go on, Niccolo. What else?" Lorenzo's father prodded the boy.

"I saw him jump into the river on Scoppio . . . ," Niccolo continued.

Signor Arrighi stood up. "What? The river?"

"I think he was trying to save time, sire," the boy answered. "He had Scoppio swim downstream, probably to the river road on the other side of the wall."

"Holy Mother!" Signor Arrighi knew of the tunnel under the wall, and the bars—they had been his idea. Fear filled his heart. *My son might be dead,* he thought, *and it will be my fault.*

The sound of hoofbeats broke into the father's thoughts. "What is that, Niccolo?"

"The relief column, sire—they are leaving the city." Niccolo ran to the window. "Look, there is Massimo. He's wearing armor!"

Signor Arrighi rushed out to the street just as the column was passing the armory; they were moving quickly. He looked for Massimo.

"Massimo!" he called out, then saw him. His old friend was dressed for battle; a light cuirass protected his upper body, his helmet had cheek guards, and in his gloved hand he held a lance.

"Massimo—save Lorenzo!" signor Arrighi shouted as his friend rode by. But his words were lost in the clatter of a hundred horses.

Chapter 14

"They are close, my lord, the Florentines and their German lackeys!" Lorenzo called out to the duke. He had just ridden in from his scouting mission.

"Where, son?" The duke was eager for news. "How many?"

"Just south of the clearing," the boy replied. "They were only a small scouting party and after they questioned me they rode—"

"They questioned you?"

"Yes, sire." Lorenzo told of his meeting with the enemy.

Before he had finished the duke began issuing orders. "Lieutenant, tell the captain we must get to the clearing quickly." He waved the man on, but motioned Lorenzo to remain by his side.

The column resumed its march, but at a faster pace. Scoppio wanted to break into a full gallop, but Lorenzo held him back. In minutes they were at the base of the long incline that led to the clearing. At the top their lead scout was waving frantically for them to hurry. Suddenly the soldier was engulfed in a shower of arrows. Lorenzo saw him grab at his leg and slump over in his saddle.

"Crossbows!" the captain called out. "Quickly, up the hill!" He spurred his horse into a full run.

Lorenzo, the duke, and the rest of the column followed him. *Another two hundred paces and we're there,* Lorenzo thought as he watched the other horses struggling to keep up with Scoppio.

As they reached the top of the hill Lorenzo could just make out the Florentine banners at the far side of the clearing.

The duke saw them too. He called the captain over. "Deploy the men into a defensive formation. They out-number us, but I'm sure we can hold them off until the relief party appears. Captain, our scout—was he badly injured?"

"No, sire. The bowmen were a long way off; the arrows were spent. It was a minor wound." The captain waited for more orders.

The duke nodded, then said, "When the relief force arrives, we will make a run to the city." The captain saluted and rode off. The duke turned to Lorenzo. "Stay by my side until we are within the city's walls."

"Yes, my lord." Lorenzo could see the anger in the duke's face—directed not at him, but at the ally whose treachery had put the duke in this life-and-death situation. Lorenzo knew that such a betrayal would not go unpunished. He knew that the duke, even now, was planning his revenge.

"My lord, the Florentines are forming to charge," the captain reported.

Lorenzo watched and listened as the duke gave detailed orders to the captain. The duke's visor was up, so the boy could see his expression change from anger to one of calm. *The duke is a true warrior,* Lorenzo marveled. *He faces death like it is nothing.*

The captain ordered the dozen men armed with crossbows to the front line. They dismounted and knelt. "Do not loose your arrows until you hear my command. Aim for the closest riders."

Lorenzo looked at the sky; the sun was high. Flashes of light sparkled on the enemy helmets and spear points. The long line of Florentine and German cavalry—Lorenzo guessed their number at a hundred—slowly began to move toward their position. The boy felt his horse shudder under him. *Even Scoppio senses that something is about to happen,* he realized.

He looked at the enemy and waited—waited for fear to grip him. Death was coming; it was charging at him. Armored knights holding lances of fire—and he, without armor, without weapons, almost like his nightmare. But then, off to his side, he heard the duke.

"Courage, my son."

Lorenzo looked straight ahead; he could make out the detail on the enemy armor. *Holy Mother, protect me,* he prayed.

"Crossbows, now!" cried the captain.

Chapter 15

Lorenzo watched in horror and fascination as the bow-men's arrows hit their targets. Men and horses hurtled to the ground, the sound of their screams filling his head, then, the roar of metal smashing into metal as the enemy knights slammed into the duke's men.

The duke's knights stood their ground. The hand-to-hand fighting was brutal. The smell of blood was heavy in the air. Scoppio pawed the ground, his nostrils dilating, foam spilling from his mouth; it was all Lorenzo could do to keep him in check. The duke drew his sword and started forward; two of his knights struggled to keep him from plunging into the fight.

Suddenly the right side of the Florentine line broke away from the fighting and rode off toward the road. Lorenzo watched them. "God be praised," he shouted. "The relief column—my lord, look!"

The duke turned. Maroon and gold banners fluttered

brightly above the fast-moving troop of soldiers. Cheers rang out from the duke's escort as they saw the rescue party. The captain shouted an order. His men quickly retreated, then reformed into two lines around the duke. They raced for the road.

The enemy followed at their heels, trying desperately to get to the duke. Lorenzo tried to stay close to his leader. Out of the corner of his eye he saw an enemy archer break away from his ranks and dash forward. He was riding hard; in seconds he had passed them. Lorenzo shouted a warning, but he was too late. The soldier, a blond, bareheaded boy, raised his crossbow and shot.

His aim was deadly. The arrow struck the duke's horse in the neck just above its armor. The horse reared. Mortally wounded, the charger lunged to one side, then crashed to the ground, pinning the duke under him.

Lorenzo reined in Scoppio and jumped to the ground. "Quick, get the duke out. Put him on Scoppio," he shouted at the duke's guard, trying to be heard above the noise of battle.

Two of his soldiers had the duke by the shoulders, but the weight of the horse was too great. Lorenzo grabbed the fallen horse's bridle and pulled with all his strength. It was just enough to free the duke's leg.

"Hurry, get him on my horse!" the boy urged the men as they lifted their wounded leader up onto Scoppio. Lorenzo was frantic; he saw the enemy pressing in on all sides. They had broken through the lines at several places.

Fierce sword fights raged all around them. As he climbed up behind the duke something wet hit him in the face. He looked down. The front of his shirt was covered in blood. "Oh, my God, I've been hit!" he cried. Then he saw it. Wedged between him and the duke was a severed hand. Horrified, he swept it away. He grabbed the reins and dug his heels hard into Scoppio. The horse shot forward. The duke's escort raced to keep up with him.

Lorenzo had Scoppio in a full gallop. Up ahead, as he

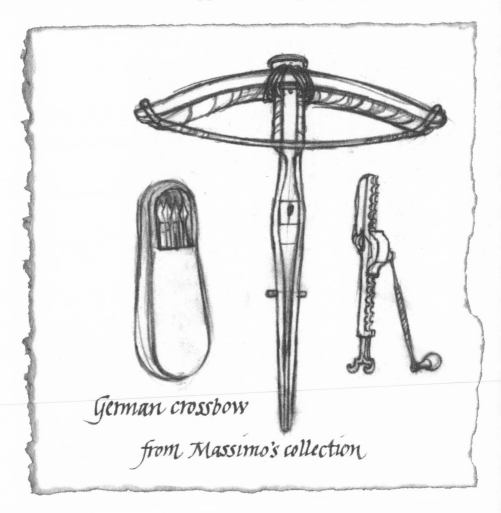

German crossbow
from Massimo's collection

peered over the duke's hunched shoulders, he could see the city walls. *We are going to make it,* he thought. About two hundred paces ahead, a soldier from the relief party pulled out from his post along the road. He turned toward Lorenzo and the duke.

What is he doing? thought the boy. *His lance is down and he's charging straight at us.*

The rider hurtled toward them; Lorenzo felt panic rising in his throat. Then he saw the rider's face.

"Massimo!" he shouted. "What are—"

The old soldier sped past without turning his head. A second later Lorenzo heard a crash of metal and a scream. A riderless horse with Florentine colors went galloping off to his right. The boy turned quickly and caught a glimpse of Massimo, his lance raised in triumph, riding hard behind him.

A quarter of a mile to the city, Lorenzo guessed. He could make out figures lining the top of the wall. He thought he could hear cheering, but the sounds of battle were still too loud.

The south gate swung open. More armed men rode out to guard their entry, but they weren't needed. They were home, and the duke was safe.

Chapter 16

The air in the armory was so heavy Lorenzo could hardly breathe. The weather had turned warmer and the forges were operating day and night. Only three weeks had passed since his narrow escape, but the duke had wasted no time in preparing for his revenge against the ally who had betrayed him. Lorenzo still remembered the look on the duke's face when he first learned of the treachery. Now it was the duke's turn. His subjects, too, wanted justice. Men from the city and elsewhere in the duke's realm came to join his army. Most of them needed arms, and the Arrighi armory was working hard to provide them.

Lorenzo put his hammer down and went outside for fresh air. His father and Massimo were there talking together.

"Here, son." Signor Arrighi handed the boy a goblet of water.

Lorenzo took a long drink. In the weeks since the ambush his father had said nothing about his ride to warn the duke, a ride that could have cost him his life. Even at the festival of thanksgiving signor Arrighi had said nothing. But he did notice his father's tears when the duke proclaimed Lorenzo Arrighi "a hero of the city" for his actions during the ambush. So to respect his father's silence, Lorenzo too said nothing.

"Lorenzo, my boy, what is that interesting armor you are working on?" Massimo took his godson by the arm and

New breastplate design for the duke

walked to the boy's forge. Signor Arrighi followed them.

"Yes, son, what is that?" His father picked up Lorenzo's work and examined it in the light of the forge. "Massimo, look at this breastplate. Is it not like the ceremonial cuirass the duke wore when he was attacked?"

"Renato, you are right, but . . ." Massimo seemed as confused as Lorenzo's father.

"You did not authorize this work, Massimo?" the elder Arrighi asked. Both men looked at the boy. They waited for an answer.

Lorenzo was embarrassed. "The duke asked me to make it, at the palace on the day of the festival. His father's armor served him so well during the fight, he wanted a new battle-ready version—with all of the latest improvements."

"Why didn't you tell me, son?" his father asked.

Lorenzo could hear the hurt feelings in his father's voice. And he understood. He too had thought it odd that the duke would speak directly to him; it was unheard of.

"I am sorry, Father; I meant to. But everything has been so busy here, I—"

His father interrupted him. "No matter, my son. If the duke requested it, that is enough." He turned to his friend. "Massimo, I would like to speak with you." The two walked a short distance away from Lorenzo's forge.

The noise in the armory was loud, as usual. Still, Lorenzo tried to catch the conversation between the two men. He sensed it had to do with the matter of the duke's armor. He too felt there was more to the duke's request than just a suit of armor. But what? Did his father know? Did Massimo? He listened.

"What is happening here, Massimo?" he heard his father ask. "Tell me, old friend, you are good at such things. Why did the duke go directly to . . ."

A loud noise drowned out the next words, but Lorenzo could guess what they were. He looked around the shop. *If it could only quiet down,* he wished, *I might be able to hear Massimo's answer.*

The boy watched Massimo. The man seemed to be thinking about his answer. His father appeared impatient. Did Massimo know anything? He wasn't saying anything, yet—*wait!* Lorenzo saw Massimo put his arm on his father's shoulder; his expression was very serious. Lorenzo strained to hear what he had to say.

"You are not going to like . . ." A piece of armor dropped; Lorenzo missed some of Massimo's words. ". . . you will be faced with the most heart wrenching decision of your life."

The shop had suddenly become very quiet; a messenger from the duke had arrived. And everyone—the messenger, the other armorers, and Lorenzo—had heard Massimo's every word.

Chapter 17

Lorenzo sat bareback on Scoppio in the shade of a building. It was still early in the day, but the sun was already hot. The sound of church bells echoed from every corner of the cathedral square. Today the duke was going to war.

The duke had declared war against his former ally, Count Barzio. The count's property had been raided, his vineyards burned. But the three-week campaign against the traitor had failed to flush him out of hiding. Count Barzio had, so far, refused to leave the safety of his city.

"The man is not only a traitor, he is a coward. And I will not rest until he is crushed." Lorenzo remembered the exact words of the duke. He, his father, and Massimo had been at the palace when the duke announced his decision to go to war. The duke had been humiliated by the count's treachery. His enemies would never fear him again if he did not retaliate. Now only a full-scale war could do that, and Lorenzo wanted to be part of it. But his father would have none of it.

They argued for three days. In the end his father won.

Lorenzo watched the booths and tents spring up around the square. He usually looked forward to these festivals, but not this day; his thoughts were only on his frustration and what he must do.

The square began to fill with people. A small crowd gathered in front of a puppet theater. One of the puppets looked like Count Barzio, another like the duke. Each time the "duke" knocked down the "count" the audience let out a roar of approval. "Again!" they shouted. "Again!"

It was a bitter sight to Lorenzo. It only made him more furious at his father. He was tired of being protected, of being treated like a child. He knew he was old enough to go to war; he had proved it—he had saved the duke. The mercenary who killed the duke's horse—Lorenzo could still see the soldier's face—couldn't have been much older than himself.

Scoppio was getting restless. The crowd had grown and was pressing in on them. Lorenzo backed his horse into a shallow alcove to settle him down.

"Good boy, Scoppio." Lorenzo leaned over his neck to adjust the forelock that fell over the top strap of the bridle. The boy's face brushed against Scoppio's mane. Suddenly his chest tightened and a cry welled up in his throat. He fought to choke it back, but his emotions overwhelmed him. He buried his face in Scoppio's mane, but the familiar smell of the horse only added to his grief.

Trumpets blared. Lorenzo looked up. A loud cheer

rose from the crowd. The duke and his escort were waiting to enter the square. The crowd moved aside. Their cheers grew louder as the duke walked to the foot of the cathedral steps and knelt before the bishop.

The ceremonies began with a solemn blessing. Then the bishop led the people in prayers for the city, the duke, and for victory. When at last the final "amen" had drifted away, the duke rose and addressed his subjects.

Lorenzo wiped the tears from his face. It was time to do what he knew he had to do. But he waited; the duke had begun speaking.

"Today I go to reclaim the honor of our great city. Today I go to destroy the traitor who has stolen our honor. And today I go to fight, and—if God wills—to die to protect our freedom."

The people's thunderous shout startled Scoppio; he skittered about on the smooth stones of the piazza, scattering a few of the onlookers.

"Easy, boy, easy." Lorenzo tightened the reins. The duke had finished and was about to leave the steps. He turned Scoppio toward the cathedral and began walking through the crowd. Some of those closest to the boy recognized him.

"It's Lorenzo, the boy who saved the duke," they shouted. "Make way!" A few reached out to touch him and his horse. The movement of the crowd caught the duke's attention. He looked in Lorenzo's direction.

The boy did not look at the duke. He pulled Scoppio to

Scoppio at age seven – he is ready!

a stop and dismounted. Leading the horse by the reins he walked the rest of the way to the church steps. The crowd had grown silent. Everyone watched as the boy went down on one knee before their ruler.

"My lord, Your Excellency, may I speak?" Lorenzo hardly recognized the sound of his own voice; it was small, thin, almost inaudible.

The duke, bareheaded, resplendent in a cloak of maroon and gold, nodded his permission. The boy, head bowed, did not see the duke's signal. He remained silent, waiting.

"Yes, Lorenzo, you may speak." The duke's voice was soft, kind.

The boy raised his head and spoke, his voice stronger with each word. "My lord—my wish is to fight by your side—"

A murmur rose from the people closest to the steps. The duke raised his hand for silence. "Go on, my boy," he said.

". . . But I have been forbidden to do so." He paused. "I am told I am too young. So—" the boy fought to control himself "—in my stead, I give you my warhorse." Quickly he led Scoppio up the steps and handed the reins to the duke.

Without waiting to be dismissed or looking at the horse—at the magnificent creature he had raised from a colt—Lorenzo walked swiftly down the steps and plunged into the cheering crowd. Not for one second longer could he bear the pain of being there.

For a minute the duke stood watching and listening, as the crowd's shouts of approval followed the boy through the square. Then he signaled his aide to saddle the horse.

At the far side of the square Lorenzo paused to calm his feelings. He knew that his actions would bring embarrassment to his father. But the conflict of his loyalties had become a heavy burden. *What else could I have done to show my devotion?* he wondered. He looked once more at the crowd and left the square.

The people had turned back toward the duke. "Long live the duke!" they chanted over and over. The duke climbed into the saddle. Scoppio, sensing a strange rider, pranced about for a few seconds before his new master walked him slowly into the square. The crowd closed in behind the duke, shouting their praise and praying for his safety. When the duke reached the edge of the square, he paused for a last look at his city and his people. He turned slowly in the saddle, searching for Lorenzo, but could not find him.

The people responded with more shouts and chants while children threw flowers in the duke's path. Among their voices he heard one that rose above the others: "Long live Lorenzo!" shouted a young woman. Others picked it up, and soon the entire crowd had added the boy's name to their litany of praise. And, for the first time since he had lost his son, the duke felt hope in his heart.

Chapter 18

Lorenzo worked feverishly at his forge. The harsh sounds and hectic pace of the workshop kept him from thinking of his horse, of worrying over his decision to give Scoppio to the duke.

When he heard of the duke's progress against the traitor, Count Barzio, he was even more upset. *I should be there, I should be there,* he shouted to himself, pounding on a piece of armor until Roberto, his apprentice, called him by name.

His father came by and left a list of arms the duke needed. Most were replacements for weapons lost or stolen during the past two weeks of heavy fighting outside the count's city.

Father and son avoided each other if they could. After their argument they had settled into a truce, but neither believed it would last. His father knew that Lorenzo had not given up his dream of being a knight.

"A herald from the duke—he has news of the war!"

Roberto pulled on Lorenzo's arm. "Hurry, he's at the square in front of the church."

The boy threw off his apron, grabbed his tunic, and ran from the workshop.

A light rain was falling, so the stones were slippery and the ground was muddy, but Lorenzo hardly noticed. By the time he'd reached the square, a crowd had gathered around the herald. The messenger, a young boy sitting astride an old horse, raised a brass horn to his lips and blew a short fanfare to get everyone's attention.

"Citizens, His Excellency, the duke, sends his greetings. The war is going well. The cowardly traitor Count Barzio has finally been flushed from his hiding place." The crowd shouted their approval. The herald continued. "The count is ready to face our army on the field of battle." Another cheer erupted. "By noon tomorrow our city's honor will have been avenged. God save the duke, God save our city!"

With the people's cheers following him, the herald rode off toward the armory. He saw Lorenzo and stopped.

"Signor Arrighi," the boy called out.

Lorenzo couldn't help resenting the herald. *He's younger than I and goes to war and I'm forced to stay behind like a coward.* The anger at his father welled up in him again.

"I have a message from the duke." The herald pulled a small roll of parchment from his leather pouch. "It lists the weapons the army needs most urgently. An escort is ready to take them to the duke's camp as soon as the wagon is loaded."

Lorenzo grabbed the list and took off for the armory at a run. Over his shoulder he shouted to the herald, "Tell the escort the wagon will be ready to leave within the hour."

Lorenzo raced to the stable under the armory. He took a pitchfork and banged its handle against the trapdoor in the ceiling.

Niccolo, Massimo's assistant, opened it. "What is it, Lorenzo?"

Lorenzo reached up to the trapdoor. "Here's a list of weapons the duke needs now. It's mostly lances and shields. Get as many as you can and load the wagon. Tell Roberto to harness the horses and to get ready; he's coming with me." The boy ran up the stairs to his room.

Lorenzo quickly changed out of his work clothes. He put on his heavy boots and reached for a fresh tunic. Hanging on the same hook was a leather case with his drawing supplies, the one he always carried when he traveled with his father. Without thinking, he took it and threw it over his shoulder. He hurried down the hall to the stairs that led to the stable. Massimo was waiting for him.

Massimo blocked his way to the stairs. "I'm sorry, Lorenzo; you cannot go."

The boy tried to push past the shop master, but the older man grabbed the boy's arm. Lorenzo winced from the tight grip. "I'm going, Massimo. Don't try to stop me."

"That is a war zone, Lorenzo. Mercenaries are everywhere. Your father has forbidden it." He looked pleadingly at his godson.

Lorenzo pulled his arm from his godfather's hold. He looked into Massimo's eyes; his pulse was pounding in his ears. "I'm going."

He ran down the stairs; Roberto was waiting, the wagon was loaded. Their escort, led by one of the duke's officers, had arrived. Lorenzo signaled to the lieutenant that they were ready.

The column began to move.

Chapter 19

"Lorenzo, stop the wagon." The lieutenant pulled up alongside the boy and reined in his horse.

"Why are we stopping, Lieutenant? It's getting late," Lorenzo asked. They had been traveling for hours and he was eager to get to their destination.

"We are only a mile or so from the duke's camp. But the woods around here are swarming with mercenaries." The lieutenant paused and looked at the surrounding trees as if he expected to see an enemy soldier at that very moment. "These foreign hirelings are more interested in bounty than in fighting. The arms might tempt them and I can't risk losing this wagon. I've sent ahead for reinforcements. They won't be long in coming." The soldier wheeled his horse about and rode to the back of the column.

Roberto had fallen asleep sitting up. Lorenzo watched him enviously. *I could use a rest*, he thought, *but not until I deliver these arms and find Scoppio.* He looked around. Twilight was approaching and the shadows in the woods were deepening. *If we're attacked here,* he thought, *we won't have a chance.*

His gloomy thoughts vanished at the sound of horses riding hard toward them. *Friend or enemy?* he wondered. The dwindling light made it difficult to identify the troop of soldiers riding toward them.

"Lorenzo, good to see you." Sergeant Bellini, cheerful as usual, pulled up beside the wagon.

"Sergeant, you're a welcome sight." Lorenzo greeted the oldest member of the duke's personal guard; the faithful veteran had known Lorenzo since he was a child.

"The duke sent me to escort you personally. He wants to see you." He looked into the wagon. "And he will welcome these; we are in short supply." For a moment, his usual smile deserted him, but he recovered and waved Lorenzo forward. "Within the hour you will see the duke and your horse." He rode to the head of his troops.

Roberto, a bit groggy but awake, took the reins, leaving Lorenzo with his thoughts, and they were not comforting.

Something about the sergeant's brief show of concern unsettled Lorenzo. *Was victory in doubt?* he wondered. *Impossible. The duke has never been defeated; his army is experienced and very well armed.* That brought his father to mind. He was thinking of what he would tell him on his return, when a hard bump nearly jolted him out of the wagon.

"Easy, Roberto. Watch where you're going."

"Quiet! Everyone, quiet!" The lieutenant raised his hand. The column came to a halt. They were in the thickest part of the woods. Ahead a hundred paces or so, the tree line thinned out. Silhouetted against the fading light, a cavalry unit moving at a fast pace was crossing their path.

"Who are—" Lorenzo slapped a hand over Roberto's mouth. The lieutenant looked at them sharply.

Finally the last of the horsemen passed out of their view. The officer waited another minute or two, then waved the column forward.

"That was the enemy, Roberto. Sorry if I hurt you, but if they'd heard us, we might all be dead now. Did you see? There must have been over a hundred soldiers in that troop. That's not a band of stragglers." Lorenzo shook his head. "The duke won't like this news."

Twenty minutes later they rolled into the duke's camp. A light rain was falling. As the two boys began unhitching the horses, squad leaders, eager for the weapons, started to unload the wagon. In the middle of all this activity Lorenzo felt a hand on his shoulder.

"Lorenzo, come with me. The duke is meeting with his field officers, but he wants to see you." Sergeant Bellini motioned for the boy to follow.

Their path wound through the camp. Groups of soldiers huddled around cook fires preparing their supper. Firelight flickered brightly over rows of armor stacked on poles—an army of disembodied knights suspended within the thickening shadows of a summer night. The sight sent a chill through the boy.

"In here, Lorenzo." Sergeant Bellini held aside the flap as the boy entered the duke's tent. The sergeant followed.

Their leader, his back to them, was leaning over a table covered with maps and colored squares of wood.

"My lord," the sergeant spoke quietly, not wanting to startle the duke. "The boy, Lorenzo, is here."

Chapter 20

The duke turned around. His face filled with pleasure at the sight of Lorenzo.

And for the first time in the boy's memory, the duke was smiling.

"Sit down, my boy. Sergeant, have my orderly bring some food and drink; Lorenzo must be hungry." The duke pulled up a stool and sat facing Lorenzo.

"Yes, my lord, thank you. It was a difficult journey." Lorenzo looked around the tent. It was plain, austere. No comforts. Only a cot, two stools, a place for weapons, and the campaign table—a warrior's place.

"Lorenzo," the duke began speaking as the boy started to eat. "I had no opportunity to thank you for your gift. Scoppio is a truly fine warhorse, strong, and very well trained. Before you return you must visit him; my orderly will take you." The duke paused, waiting for Lorenzo to finish his food.

The boy had never heard the duke speak so personally. He put down his spoon. "It was my honor, Your Excellency. If I may say so, he is a worthy mount for you, my lord." Lorenzo could hardly believe his own ears; he sounded like one of the duke's courtiers. Still, he meant every word.

Sergeant Bellini appeared at the tent flap. "My lord, the officers are waiting."

"Yes, Sergeant." The duke stood up.

Lorenzo snapped to his feet, almost spilling his soup.

"Lorenzo, convey my gratitude to your father; his armor serves us well." He turned to the sergeant. "Tomorrow at first light, Lorenzo will take his wagon with some of our wounded back to the city. See that an escort is ready." Then the duke reached out and put his hand on the boy's head. "Go with God . . . my son."

Lorenzo, stunned by the duke's display of affection, lost his voice and his manners. Luckily the sergeant was beside him. He took his arm and led him out of the tent.

Once outside the boy looked at the sergeant. "I can't believe it. I didn't say good-bye—or thank you. I've insulted the duke."

The sergeant, a wise old soldier, and perhaps, the person closest to the duke, reassured him. "Trust me, my boy, you have insulted no one. How could you think that? Knowing what the duke has planned for you as soon as . . ."

"What plan?" The surprise in the boy's voice and the look on his face silenced the sergeant. "What has the duke planned for me?" Lorenzo repeated.

Sergeant Bellini shook his head from side to side. "Lorenzo Arrighi, I am very sorry. You must forgive me. I was certain your father had spoken of it to you, but . . ."

"Spoken of what, Sergeant? I have been told nothing. What is it that I should know?" The boy was pleading with the soldier.

"I have said too much as it is. When you return to the city tomorrow, ask your father. I am sorry; I must see to my men." The soldier turned and left abruptly.

The duke's orderly had been waiting to one side. Now he motioned Lorenzo to follow him. The boy, his head still spinning from the sergeant's words, had almost forgotten about Scoppio. But in minutes he found himself in the midst of dozens of horses. All of them were being prepared for the next day's battle. Each of the knights' mounts was being cleaned and curried. Hooves were being checked. Some horses were having their manes and tails braided. Every set of horse armor and harness was being polished and oiled. Lorenzo knew that the knights were tending to their armor in the same way elsewhere in the camp.

"Signor Arrighi," the orderly said, "Scoppio is here, somewhere, perhaps at the blacksmith's. I'm sure you'll find him. I must return to the duke's tent." The orderly pointed to a cluster of wagons about fifty paces away. "Your wagon is over there with the other transport. There is fresh straw for bedding."

Night had come, but light from the encircling campfires and torches made it easy for the boy to make his way through the milling animals and their handlers. The battle was only hours away and Lorenzo could sense the excitement and energy building. He could feel it in the pit of his stomach.

A warm muzzle brushed the back of his neck. Lorenzo spun around. Scoppio had found him. He threw his arms around the horse's neck and squeezed hard. Scoppio whinnied and tossed his head. Lorenzo grabbed the bridle and pulled the horse's head close to his own. "I miss you, boy," he murmured. Scoppio snorted softly. The boy stepped back and took the bridle in both hands. He held Scoppio's head very still and looked into his eyes.

"Tomorrow is your first big battle. You will carry the duke to victory. You will make me proud. And—" his voice faltered "—you will not get hurt. Do you hear me, Scoppio? You will not . . ."

"Signor Arrighi, excuse me, I must take the horse." A stable hand took Scoppio by the halter strap and led him to his stall.

As Lorenzo watched his horse being led away, the unease he'd been feeling all day became one dreaded premonition: If he left before the battle, he would never see Scoppio again.

Chapter 21

The explosion jolted Lorenzo awake. From his straw bed under the wagon he could see fires breaking out around the camp. He grabbed Roberto and pulled the sleeping apprentice from beneath the wagon.

"Roberto, wake up! We've got to move. Get the team. I'll fix the harness. Hurry!" Lorenzo checked to see if any flames had burned the wagon.

"Signor Arrighi," a soldier called out, "we have to leave as soon as the wounded are loaded. Catapults have been bombarding us; fires are burning all over the camp." The soldier stammered. He was young and scared.

"Is the duke all right?" Lorenzo resisted the urge to fall to the ground as another fireball went flying over their heads.

"Yes, but he's ordered everyone to their posts."

"Where are the wounded?" A huge fir tree burst into flames. Lorenzo had to shout over the noise of the fire. "And our escort?"

The soldier pointed to a column coming toward them. About fifteen or twenty wounded led by another soldier, slowly began climbing into the wagon. The young soldier went to help them, leaving Lorenzo and Roberto to finish harnessing the team.

Lorenzo reached out and pulled Roberto close to him. "Listen, Roberto, a few minutes after we reach the trail, I'm getting off. They must not know I'm gone until you're too far along the road to turn back. Understand?"

Roberto stared back at Lorenzo. "You must be mad, Lorenzo. Your father will be—"

Lorenzo grabbed the apprentice by both shoulders. "Do you understand?" he repeated.

Roberto nodded.

The two boys climbed onto the wagon seat; Lorenzo signaled to the soldiers that they were ready. The escort rode ahead about fifty paces, then waved to the wagon to follow.

Groans sounded from the wounded as the wagon bounced and bumped over the ruts in the trail. It was just before dawn, and except for the fires burning in the camp there wasn't much light. Lorenzo could barely see. He waited until the wagon had gone another hundred paces then climbed over its side and dropped to the ground. With a few strides he was into the woods and making his way back in the direction of the duke's camp.

Keeping away from the road he followed the high ground to a ridge that overlooked a wide plain: the battle

Massimo has promised to help me make this armor

site. Lorenzo looked up at the sky. The sun had just risen, its light and warmth hidden behind a thick bank of low-hanging clouds. The boy smelled the air. *Rain is coming,* he thought.

Below him the two armies were already moving into position. Early morning mist still lingered at ground level, turning the soldiers into ghostly specters as they formed their lines at opposite ends of the battlefield. Every now and then the dull gray early light was set aglow by a fireball flying overhead and crashing into one of the staging areas. Lorenzo was relieved to see the duke's catapults in action.

He began to see himself traveling back to the city before nightfall in the company of a victorious army.

Over the next hour the ranks of both armies swelled. Lorenzo had studied all the duke's campaigns; he guessed that in the coming battle, the duke would use one of his favorite tactics. A small but heavily armed troop of mounted knights would be sent straight into the center of the enemy line. As these experienced fighters spread terror and confusion, the duke would follow them with infantry. Finally, as the enemy tried to encircle the duke's forces in the center, he would send in two columns of light cavalry on both flanks of the enemy. Then the enemy would be pinned between two forces and would have to retreat or die fighting. The count's army would be doomed. And when Lorenzo saw the count's knights move into position, he was sure he was right. They were no match for the duke's men.

Lorenzo looked at the sky again. The clouds were more threatening, but there was no rain yet. He expected the duke to attack at any minute. He listened for the brass trumpets that always signaled the first assault. He could already see the banners of the duke's elite corps of knights as they moved forward through the waiting ranks of infantry. They formed a column of steel, relentless and invincible—all Arrighi armor. He felt an enormous surge of pride. For the first time he really understood why the house of Arrighi was, in his father's words, "the sword and shield of their city." He couldn't wait for the battle to begin.

Chapter 22

A break in the clouds gave the sun a chance to illuminate the battlefield. Scoppio, resplendent in armor and gold saddle-cloth, proudly carried the duke onto the field. For a fleeting moment Lorenzo felt anger at not being the one astride the awesome warhorse; then he remembered his loyalty to the duke. *Today, Scoppio, you will make me proud,* he thought.

The duke's emissary of mercy to the traitorous Count Barzio rode back from his meeting with the count's envoy. Lorenzo knew the duke's offer of clemency in exchange for the count's admission of guilt and forfeiture of land would be refused. Events had gone too far; only blood would satisfy the two men's rage. And as if to signal the end of any hope for peace, the sun once again slipped behind the thickening cloud cover. Lorenzo looked up; still no rain, but it was only a matter of time.

Then came the sound he was waiting for, the blare of trumpets echoing across the plain, followed by a hair-raising battle cry from the duke's army. The knights began their advance. Row upon row of magnificent armored knights urged their chargers into the no-man's-land that separated the two armies.

Another blast from the horns and the horses went into a slow and determined canter. Lorenzo held his breath as the horses' great strides ate up the distance between the two armies. Then, with only two hundred paces separating the two forces, the duke's cavalry broke into a full gallop. Even from his site above the plain Lorenzo could feel the power of the charge; he could imagine the terror felt by the enemy on the front line. The count's cavalry counter-charged. Arrows filled the air. The distance between the charging knights narrowed and they lowered their lances. Lorenzo's mouth was open; he was screaming. Thirty paces—ten—the sound of collision cascaded over the field, driving out the sound of his own voice and sending hundreds of birds shrieking into the sky.

Bloody carnage filled the plain. Splintered lances and shattered shields exploded into the air as riders and horses tumbled over themselves in a futile effort to escape the deadly force of the duke's cavalry. In less than a minute the knights had broken through the count's cavalry and were creating havoc among the enemy infantry.

Again the duke's trumpets sounded. His infantry, eager to earn their share of the victory, charged across the field at full speed, some pausing only to pursue the count's unhorsed knights. It was a slaughter.

Lorenzo's heart was pounding; the duke was on his way to a great victory. The celebrations would last for days. He saw the duke order the two columns of light cavalry from his flanks to attack the enemy from both sides. That would finish the count.

Lorenzo thought he heard the trumpets sound one more time, but it wasn't the horns. He looked skyward. Flashes of lightning filled the darkened horizon and thunder boomed above the battlefield. Gusts of wind swept across the fighting men; debris swirled through their ranks. Then with a

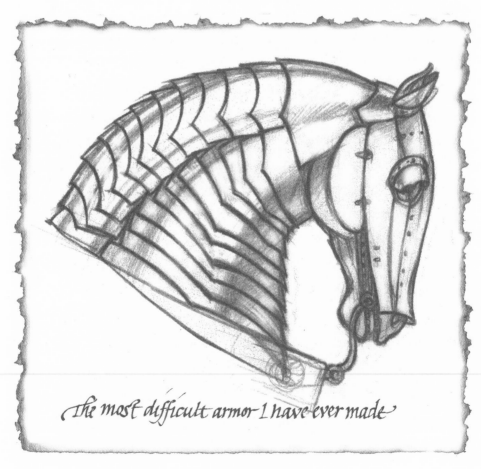

The most difficult armor I have ever made

shocking suddenness, sheets of water poured down upon them. Lorenzo was instantly soaked. The ground beneath him turned to mud and rivulets of water ran down the side of the ridge, changing the grassy plain into a quagmire. Horses and men lost their footing, the ones in heavy armor suffering the most.

Lorenzo searched for cover. He retreated from the top of the ridge to the thick brush at the edge of the tree line. As he searched for shelter his eye caught some movement about fifty paces farther along the ridge. It was a column of men and horses. Lorenzo recognized them; they were the foreign light cavalry. They had dismounted and were carefully leading their horses down the slippery slopes of the ridge. He crept to the rim of the ridge to get a clearer view of the maneuver.

With a sickening shock of understanding Lorenzo grasped what they were trying to do—capture the duke. Panic pounded in his chest; with the heavy rain, and visibility reduced to a few paces, the mercenaries would be on the duke's position before he and his guard knew it. And there was nothing he could do. In between gusts of wind and rain Lorenzo saw the mud steal the advantage from the duke's forces. The knights were forced to dismount. Fighting on foot, the knights would be unable to help the duke. When the mercenaries attacked, he would have only his personal guard to protect him.

The foreigners had reached the plain; they remounted. They were only two hundred paces from their objective.

Lorenzo watched in horror. He hated the mercenaries. They had no loyalties, no honor; to them the duke was only a prize to be taken, then auctioned to the highest bidder.

Lorenzo stood up. Rain lashed his face. He could barely see the duke's position; the two forces were fighting hand-to-hand. The duke's guard was outnumbered four to one. A trumpet sounded; it was the call to retreat. Lorenzo sank to his knees. His heart knew something terrible had happened to the duke.

Chapter 23

Gradually the rain ended. Lorenzo fearfully raised himself from the ground to face the deserted battlefield. It took all his courage. The plain was littered with the ghastly remains of the conflict. He forced his eyes to where the fighting had taken place. Slowly he searched the ground looking for any sign of the duke or Scoppio. Without realizing it his lips kept repeating over and over, *Holy Mother, let Scoppio be safe.* Then his heart stopped. Scoppio was down—there was no mistaking that white form; it stood out in stark contrast from its mud-splattered surroundings.

The boy threw himself down the rain-slicked slope, sliding and falling in his haste to reach the battlefield. His mind shut out all thoughts of death; he held fiercely to the hope that Scoppio still lived. He reached flat ground and kept running. He stumbled over something and fell headlong in the mud. As Lorenzo got to his knees he glanced down. A boot had tripped him—then with a gasp he saw the leg attached to it. Severed just above the knee, it lay near the corpse of a horse, one of Count Barzio's cavalry mounts. Lorenzo shook the image off and kept running. He heard something; he held his breath. He heard it again; a horse whinnied. Was it Scoppio? Were his senses playing tricks on him?

Lorenzo stopped and looked in the direction of the sound. It came from the place where he'd seen the white horse. *Thank God!* He tried to run faster, but the debris on the ground was thicker here. This was where the fighting had been heaviest. He had to go around more dead horses, broken lances, shields . . . bodies. They wore the armor of the mercenaries. Whatever had happened to the duke, his men had taken a heavy toll on the foreign cavalry. He stepped carefully over the corpses. The sun had come out and a thick mist was rising from the wet earth. He was suddenly enveloped in fog; he couldn't see ten paces in any direction. He listened for the horse and thought he heard a snorting sound. He groped his way toward it. He stumbled over another casualty, but this time it was one of the duke's men. The soldier was lying facedown. Lorenzo hated the sight of a brave man with his face buried in mud. He gently rolled the soldier over onto his back. The boy carefully cleaned off what he could of the dirt covering the man's face, then pulled back in horror. He put his hands over his face and cried aloud. The sightless eyes of Sergeant Bellini stared skyward, his lips; partially opened, were unsmiling. The nausea Lorenzo had been fighting finally overcame him. A feeling of despair drained the strength from the boy as the real impact of the war suddenly hit him—the loss. The veteran he'd known for years, the duke's trusted companion, gone. The duke? Maybe dead too, and Scoppio. In less than an hour his world had collapsed. Nothing would ever be the same again. Lorenzo remained slumped over the lifeless form of the brave old soldier. Hope had deserted him.

The mist had become thicker, like a shroud. As if in a gesture of mourning, it covered the dead and mangled soldiers of two proud armies who only hours earlier had shaken the very same ground with their courage and manhood.

Lorenzo stood up, disoriented, but then he heard it—a snorting sound. He knew that sound. "Scoppio! Scoppio!" he cried. The horse answered, this time with a loud whinny of recognition. The boy turned to his left and picked his way through the sodden reminders of the fierce combat. A slight breeze parted the mist in front, and there, not ten paces away, was Scoppio—alive!

The boy flung himself to the ground at his horse's side. The poor animal was struggling to get up, but his hind legs were pinned under the corpse of another horse. "Easy, boy, easy." Lorenzo tried to calm the animal; too much more of this struggling and the horse would die of exhaustion.

Quickly he studied the situation. The dead horse was too heavy to move by himself, but . . . He got up and looked around. *There has to be one here,* he told himself. But a quick search of the area near him showed no evidence of a lance, not even a piece of one. Talking softly to calm the horse, he widened his hunt. Something shiny caught his eye and he picked it up. Massimo had once told him that a true craftsman could always recognize his own work; he was right. He turned the duke's helmet over in his hands, the making of it still fresh in his memory. But what did it mean, its lying here? Did it mean that the duke was dead? Quickly he rejected the thought.

Lorenzo fastened the helmet to the strap of his travel case and continued his search for a lance. Finally he found one, as tall as a man. He hurried back to his horse. Careful not to hurt Scoppio's legs, Lorenzo wedged the lance deep under the dead horse. Then he raised the other end until he could get his shoulder under it. *Lord, don't let the lance break,* he prayed. Very gradually he began pushing up on the lance, so intent on his task that he noticed nothing else. The mist had thinned. Other figures had appeared on the battle-field. The boy saw none of this. His concern was only for his horse.

"Come on, Scoppio, come on, boy." He was urging his horse to pull his hind legs out from under as soon as the weight of the dead horse had lifted.

The sound of high-pitched laughter startled him. He turned. Three men were running toward him, their swords held high—the mercenaries. Lorenzo tugged at the lance but it was now driven too deeply into the ground. He had no weapon, and there were three of them. He ran.

One of the foreigners was only a few strides away, and Lorenzo could see his face clearly. It was a face he recognized—it belonged to the young soldier who had killed the duke's horse during the ambush. His crossbow hung at his side, and now his target was Lorenzo.

Chapter 24

The cool pine needles were a comfort to Lorenzo. He lay, breathless and spent, facedown under a tall pine at the edge of the battlefield. He inhaled deeply, grateful for the earth's fragrance, amazed that he was still alive. He thanked God for his deliverance. He had cheated death, but only by inches. He could still hear the lethal whisper of feathers as the arrow sped past his ear. He had escaped the mercenaries, but at a great cost. They had caught Scoppio; that was the reason they had not pursued Lorenzo into the forest.

From the safety of the trees Lorenzo looked out onto the deserted battlefield. He had been so close to rescuing Scoppio. Lorenzo shook his head in disgust. He hated himself for running, but if he'd stayed he would be lying dead next to Sergeant Bellini. Lord, how he hated the mercenaries; what had the duke called them? "Cowardly dogs." *I won't let them get away,* he vowed. *I'll follow them, and I'll kill them if I have to, but they're not getting Scoppio.* His emotions brought him to his feet. He began running in the direction he'd last seen the mercenaries take Scoppio. He'd pick up their trail and follow them; somehow he'd get his horse back.

Suddenly he felt hungry. He hadn't eaten since the night before, and now he was ravenous. He searched his pockets for something, a biscuit, some cheese, but he found nothing. He looked around him. Once again his godfather came to the rescue. Massimo had not only taught him all about armor, but had insisted the boy learn how to pick wild mushrooms, saying, "A soldier must know how to live off the land." A surge of gratitude for his godfather brought tears to his eyes.

Lorenzo began a search of the forest floor. He was in luck. The recent rain had pushed up a good crop. In a few minutes he had filled the deep pockets of his tunic with a satisfying assortment of mushrooms.

All the while he kept track of the mercenaries' trail. Soon he came to the place where they had tied their other horses. Lorenzo knew that now he would be left far behind. But he could not give up; sooner or later they would stop and he would catch up.

Two hours passed and he was more tired than he cared to admit. Then he remembered another saying of Massimo's, "An exhausted soldier is no better than a dead one."

The boy selected a cool spot at the base of an old fir tree. He sat down heavily on the thick soft needles and leaned back against the trunk. The place struck Lorenzo as so gentle and peaceful he could almost believe that this terrible day had been only a bad dream.

He took a few mushrooms and began eating. Not as good as they'd be in Massimo's hands, cooked in olive oil and garlic, but they filled the emptiness in his stomach. As he savored each bite an idea for Scoppio's rescue began to take shape.

Lorenzo never even noticed when he dozed off. Only after he had been awakened by the sound of bells did he realize he'd fallen into a much-needed sleep. *Bells?* he asked himself. *What are bells doing out here?*

Cautiously he stood up and looked in the direction of the sound. The sun was low in the sky, and its rays, slanting through the trees, enchanted everything they touched.

Coming in his direction were two dark-robed figures: the source of the tinkling bells. Their hooded shapes, edged in bright sunlight, reminded him of the actors in passion plays he witnessed every Lent in the cathedral. The figures moved slowly, as if they were old or in pain. Every now and then they'd bend down, pick something up and deposit it in the folds of their garments. *They're picking mushrooms,* Lorenzo realized. He also noticed they had come from the direction taken by the mercenaries; perhaps they had even seen them.

He began walking toward them. Knowing that country folk were fearful of strangers, and not wanting to startle them, he called out in as friendly a way as he could.

At the sound of his voice the two people gave a cry

and, heedless of their harvest, began running away. Lorenzo hurried after them, eager to quiet their fears, and anxious about losing news they might have of Scoppio and his captors. He caught up to them in minutes.

"Please, good people," he called out in the most respectful voice he had. "I mean you no harm. I need your help to find my horse. Please, will you not at least speak to me?" Lorenzo stopped and waited for a reply.

One of them turned to face him. A bright band of sunlight framed the hooded cloak, casting the person's face in deep shadow. All Lorenzo could see was a thin wasted hand clutching a small bell. It shook continually. The frantic tinkling awakened some faint memory in Lorenzo—something about a warning—but of what?

The shadowy form spoke. "I beg you, kind sir, leave us alone." It was the voice of a woman, weak and raspy, and with a pleading, melancholy tone.

The very sound of it touched Lorenzo's heart. It was the voice of someone in great need. He took several steps closer. "But, signora, I have only a few questions, and perhaps I can be of some help. . . ."

The woman took her other hand from beneath the torn and rotting robes and slowly pushed back one edge of her hood until a portion of her face was exposed to the angled rays of the dying sun.

Lorenzo recoiled so violently that he fell backward to the ground, jamming the duke's helmet into his shoulder. He lay there gasping from the pain and from the shock of what he'd seen. The memory came back to him. Lepers! Lepers wore bells to warn others to keep away. He had never seen one, or known of any. Certainly not in his city. But the very word "leper" was enough to strike terror in the hearts of even the bravest men. Slowly he got up and watched the two wretched souls bravely go back to the business of finding food. *How do they do it?* he asked himself. *How do they go on living in the face of such suffering and pain?* It was beyond his understanding.

He started walking in the direction they were going; he had not lost his resolve to find Scoppio and he would let nothing, not even leprosy, stand in the way of finding him. But this time he would keep his distance. Surely the lepers would tell him if they had seen Scoppio.

At first Lorenzo thought the high-pitched scream came from a forest animal. But the reaction of the two lepers, who began running toward the sound, changed his mind. The cries, Lorenzo realized, came from a child.

"Help, Mama, Papa! Help! They have her! They're hurting her!" The shrill calls for help were coming from a small figure running toward them from a deeper part of the forest.

Lorenzo raced forward and caught up with the lepers just as the crying child reached them and fell, sobbing and talking all at once.

"What is it, my child? Where is Beatrice? Who is hurting her?" The woman collapsed to the ground in tears.

Her husband moaned and tore at his robes in the most

pitiful and horrific manner Lorenzo had ever seen. The boy sensed he was witnessing a terrible tragedy, but he had no idea what it was.

"What is happening? Tell me! I want to help!" he cried out in frustration.

"Two soldiers—foreigners—have taken Beatrice. They're hurting her." The child stood and pointed. "Back there, in the clearing—not far."

Foreigners! Whatever disgust or fear Lorenzo felt toward the lepers dissolved in the cauldron of hate that welled up within him at the mention of the mercenaries. He needed a weapon. He looked around. Ten paces away he spied a sturdy-looking tree limb. He picked it up, slammed it on the ground to test it, then turned to the child.

"Show me! Take me there. Now!"

Chapter 25

Lorenzo had always dreamed of being a knight, of finding glory and honor on the battlefield, of defending the weak and powerless. He never imagined that a family of lepers would be the answer to his prayers. He looked at the child as he ran alongside her toward the clearing. Her hood had fallen back from her face, revealing the ugly beginnings of the disease. *She is so young,* he thought. A powerful sense of sorrow overwhelmed him, driving out any thoughts except the saving of this defenseless family.

Ahead he could see the light of the clearing. He had thought of a plan, but first he had to find out something. He signaled for them to stop. "Signora," he addressed the woman, "is Beatrice your daughter?"

The woman nodded.

"Is she—does she . . . ?" Lorenzo struggled to find the right words.

But the woman knew what he was trying to ask. She

shook her head vigorously. "No, signor, it is a miracle; she has been spared . . . but she stays with us and—cares for us. . . ." The woman broke down, her thin wasted body heaving uncontrollably from the force of her grief. Now he understood the truth of the tragedy that was unfolding. This woman's beloved daughter—and savior—was about to be taken from them. She had been their only hope. Their lives, pathetic as they were, would end without her.

Sounds of screams, followed by cruel, taunting laughter, warned them that they had no time to lose. The parents reacted instinctively; they began running toward the clearing. Lorenzo blocked their path.

"Wait—listen!" He spoke in a harsh whisper. "Go around to the far side of the clearing. I'll be on this side. When you see me there, run into the clearing and make as much noise as you can. You must distract the soldiers so I can surprise them from behind. That is the only chance we have to save your daughter. Understand?"

They nodded and began moving toward the clearing, careful to stay out of sight of the soldiers.

Lorenzo first ran, then slowed to a walk, afraid of making too much noise. His club and the element of surprise were his only weapons.

He was close enough now to see what was happening. The mercenaries, confident they were alone, were taking their time with their captive. She was a young woman, older than he, with long beautiful hair that swirled around her head each time she was pushed from one captor to the

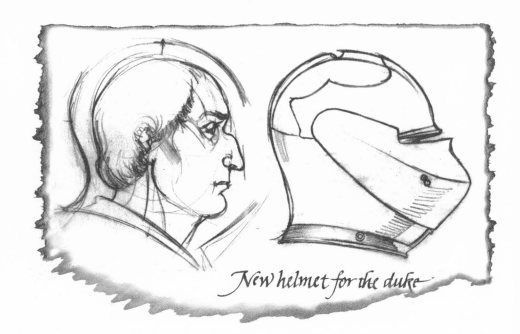

New helmet for the duke

other. Instead of tying her, they let her run free. Every time she tried to reach the freedom of the woods, they'd drag her by the hair back to the center of the clearing. Each time Lorenzo witnessed this cruel game it took all his willpower to stay hidden.

He waited and watched for a sign that the captive's family had reached their position at the far side of the clearing. He could not make a move until they were there. *And it better be soon,* he thought; *the filthy swine will soon tire of their cat and mouse game.*

Lorenzo was right. One of the soldiers suddenly threw their plaything to the ground. The other knelt down to hold her. The young woman had stopped screaming; she began to pray. She begged the Holy Mother for help—for her soul, and for her family. Lorenzo listened in agony, waiting for a sign from the far side of the clearing. He found himself praying silently along with the victim, *Blessed Virgin, help me save these poor people—please, help me!*

Finally he saw a rustling in the woods opposite him. He knew he had only seconds to surprise the soldiers. Lorenzo waved the club above his head. The family saw it. They came to the edge of the woods and just as the other soldier knelt down, they rushed into the clearing, shouting and yelling with all their strength.

The soldier who had just knelt down tried to get up, but stumbled on his own helmet. The other mercenary, still on one knee, turned toward the commotion.

Lorenzo leaped from his hiding place and raced across the clearing. With all his strength he smashed the tree branch across the back of the nearest soldier, sending him crashing to the ground. He turned to deal with the other soldier, and as he did, caught the eyes of the young woman. It was a look he would never forget.

The other soldier had drawn his sword. Lorenzo took two steps forward, raised the club over his head and brought it down on the soldier's arm. The loud crack of splintered bone, followed instantly by a piercing cry, nearly deafened Lorenzo. The enemy's sword went flying into the air, landing ten paces away. The wounded mercenary, afraid for his life, struggled toward it. Lorenzo followed him and, using both hands, swung the tree branch in a wide arc, catching the man across the shoulders with such force that he went flying headfirst into a shallow ditch. He lay there in the mud, unmoving, gasping for breath.

Seeing their chance, the family rushed to the young woman's side. They did their best to comfort her, all the while praising God for her deliverance.

Lorenzo, suddenly drained of his strength, stood over the sword. *What should I do with these animals?* he asked himself. He looked down at the sword. *Should I kill them?* He bent down to pick it up. He heard his pulse pounding in his ears; or were the sounds he thought he heard hoofbeats? He looked up. Beatrice was looking at him; no, she was looking past him. He turned.

Chapter 26

Lorenzo opened his eyes. They looked up into a noonday sun that danced and sparkled above a thick canopy of leaves. He had no idea where he was or how long he'd been there. But he sensed that something was not right, that he should lie perfectly still. That was fortunate. If he had moved, the pain in his back would have made him unconscious.

"Don't move, my son." The voice was gentle and knowing. It came from somewhere within the homespun folds of a monk's garment.

"Where am I?" Lorenzo tried to turn his head to one side, but the movement caused too much pain.

"You are among friends, with the woman you saved, and her family," the man answered.

"Who are you, Brother?" Lorenzo asked, trying to get his bearings.

"Brother Ambrose. And I am here to help you." The

monk reached behind Lorenzo and very gently raised the boy's head.

"Drink this; it will ease the pain." A new voice, light and tender came from his left. Painfully he turned to see its owner.

At that moment the sunlight chose to pour through a gap in the leafy shield; all he could see was a halo of golden brown curls that fell in waves to a point below his view.

"Here, swallow this," the voice continued. The rim of a cup touched his lips and a warm, slightly bitter liquid poured into his mouth.

He swallowed it. He felt his head being lowered. The head of curls came closer. The sun went behind a cloud, briefly transforming the harsh dark shadows of midday into the soft warm tones of dusk. He saw her face. Was she the daughter of the lepers?

"Beatrice?" His voice was little more than a whisper. He tried to focus on her features but his eyelids were becoming a burden. He could barely keep them open. Finally he gave up trying. As he drifted deeper into sleep he heard a soft voice, full of concern, asking, "Brother Ambrose, will he recover?"

Lorenzo slipped in and out of sleep. The sounds of birds, of bells, of voices urging him to drink, all merged into one long half-conscious reverie. At some point he felt himself being turned over and something soothing applied to his back. Darkness finally came, and with it a full measure of sleep for Lorenzo.

He woke up the next morning at first light. He felt stronger, but when he tried to lift himself, the pain took his breath away. *Is my back broken?* The thought frightened Lorenzo. He didn't know what had happened to him; he still didn't know where he was. In spite of the pain he forced himself up onto his elbows and looked around.

He was in some sort of campsite. Crude lean-tos were scattered about. A few figures, most wearing long tattered robes, moved slowly around the cook fires preparing the morning meal. Lorenzo realized he was in a leper camp. The realization did not terrify him as it would have a mere two days ago. As he pondered the strange turn his search for Scoppio had taken, one of the figures, a young woman, walked toward him.

She wore no outer robe, only a dress. She was young, but older than he was. Long brown curls encircled her face and were gathered loosely behind her neck. Her dress, although worn, was of a rich fabric and reminded Lorenzo of the gowns worn by the fine ladies he had seen at the duke's celebrations.

"How do you feel this morning, signor Arrighi?" The sound of her voice was familiar; it was the last voice he remembered before slipping into unconsciousness the day before. All of a sudden the boy felt embarrassed by his appearance. He looked quickly at his shirt front. Surprisingly, it was clean; so were his hands and arms. He was grateful for that.

"I . . . I feel better, signorina, thank you." Lorenzo was

trying to remember the proper words for speaking to well-born ladies. "Please forgive me, signorina, are you . . . is your name . . . ?"

"It is Beatrice, signor Arrighi." The young woman hesitated, then reached out and lightly touched his hand. "My family and I will be forever in your debt."

Lorenzo's mother had died when he was very young. His father and Massimo had raised him. From an early age he had worked alongside them and the other men in the armory. In the household the cook and the serving girl were kind and spoiled him, but always kept their distance. But this woman, her gentle voice, her pleasing smile, her warm touch—were all new and wonderful. He was enthralled, his pain forgotten. All he desired was to hear her voice and look at her face, which he was doing so intently that she became embarrassed and turned her head aside.

Realizing his bad manners, Lorenzo tried to explain. "Forgive me, signorina, I could not help staring at you. You resemble one of the portraits in my duke's palace." The image of an elegant young woman, her golden brown hair encircled with jeweled ribbons, the delicate blush on her translucent skin hinting at the warmth of her voice, floated through his memory.

"You honor me too much, signor Arrighi—"

"Please, signorina," Lorenzo interrupted, "my name is Lorenzo, and in truth you are very—"

"Let me check your wound, Lorenzo." Beatrice, hoping to change the subject, carefully helped the boy onto his stomach. She raised his shirt and began applying a warm salve.

"Signorina, how badly am I hurt? I must know. Is my back broken?" Lorenzo spoke through the pain; the treatment hurt in spite of her careful touch.

"The Lord was with us all that day, Lorenzo." Beatrice spoke softly as she finished dressing the boy's wound. She watched with concern as Lorenzo insisted on turning himself over.

"What did happen to me after . . ." Lorenzo stopped speaking; he realized what he was asking. *How could I be so stupid? She should not be reminded of that horrible day. What is wrong with me?* He felt his face turn red with shame.

Wishing to rescue Lorenzo from his own discomfort, Beatrice quickly returned to the subject of his wound. "Do you know what saved your life, Lorenzo? The helmet hanging on your back. It deflected the mercenary's sword just enough. It left an ugly bruise and it will hurt for days, but nothing is broken." She picked up the helmet and handed it to him.

Lorenzo turned it over in both hands; he ran his fingers over the dent. The helmet brought back so many memories—of the armory, his father, Massimo. He suddenly realized that his life there seemed remote, in the distant past, yet only a few days ago he had left it with a wagon load of arms for the duke. He turned to ask her another question. She was crying quietly.

"No, signorina, no, don't . . ." Lorenzo pleaded with

her to stop crying. He felt responsible. He should never have brought up what must be horrible memories.

Beatrice took her hands from her face. "These are only tears of gratitude, Lorenzo." She was smiling. "That was truly a day filled with miracles. First, like an avenging angel, you saved me and my family. Then the helmet saved you from being killed by the foreigner on the white warhorse, and finally—"

"Wait, please, signorina. You said the foreigner was riding a white horse. Did it have gold and maroon trappings? And the rider—was he young, blond?" Lorenzo had lifted himself all the way to a sitting position.

She nodded yes to both his questions.

"Then what happened? Did you see where the rider went?" The boy pressed Beatrice for details. The horse had to be Scoppio. But where had he been taken?

Trying to calm Lorenzo, she continued, "When you were struck, I thought you'd been killed. When I realized you were still alive, I gathered my family around you to protect you. I knew the fear of leprosy would keep the foreigner away. Then another miracle occurred. While the mercenary was seeing to his companions, Brother Ambrose came upon us; he had been hoping to take us here to this camp. He had potions and medicines for the very sick. He even offered some to the foreigner for his comrades' wounds." Beatrice paused; Lorenzo saw her eyes begin to fill with tears.

"What is it, Beatrice?" Lorenzo hated seeing her

A Franciscan brother

unhappy. "Did the mercenary try to harm the monk?"

The young woman, her head lowered, was silent for a while. Lorenzo grew more concerned. He was about to speak when she lifted her head and looked at him. Her eyes were sad and questioning.

"Help me to understand, Lorenzo." She turned slowly, looking at the campsites around them. The sick had risen by now; some were eating, others were trying as best they could to comfort the more seriously ill of their companions.

"Is there not enough suffering and sadness in this world? What did my parents and my little sister do to deserve this horrible affliction? When I asked Brother Ambrose, he said it was God's way of testing our faith."

"Like the story of Job," Lorenzo added.

She nodded. "And as difficult as it is, I can accept that, and pray that God in his mercy will deliver them from their suffering. But why must men add to all the miseries of life by their fighting and killing and cruelty?"

Lorenzo could understand her. When he had looked into the lifeless eyes of Sergeant Bellini, he too had wondered at the senselessness of his death. But he had no answer for her question—or his.

Beatrice seemed to regret her question. Not waiting for an answer she left to get him breakfast. When she returned to feed him some warm gruel, she didn't speak. *Perhaps,* Lorenzo imagined, *she thinks she has insulted me and my family.*

When he had finished eating, she gave him more of the bitter drink for his pain. She helped him lower his head. "Sleep, Lorenzo. When you are well enough to travel, I promise, we will help you get your horse."

Lorenzo immediately wanted to hear more, but the potion was already taking effect. He was getting groggy; the pain was receding and his eyes were starting to close.

The last thing he heard was, "Be patient, Lorenzo. Don't worry. I know where Scoppio is."

Chapter 27

Twice a day, sometimes more, Massimo painfully climbed the steep wooden stairs to the tower that rose above the armory. On each visit, he searched the valley road that stretched southward to the scene of the duke's last battle. And every time, after an hour or so, the master armorer would return to his forge disappointed.

That morning had begun in fog. Lorenzo's godfather decided to forgo his usual ascent; his right leg had been particularly painful the previous night, and although he would never admit to it, he was beginning to lose hope that he would ever see his godson again. Nevertheless, a tiny voice kept prodding him to go to the tower. *Am I turning into a superstitious old fool?* he asked himself. As the morning wore on, and the fog lessened, the voice grew more insistent.

"All right, I'll go!" he said aloud as he threw his hammer onto his workbench. His assistant, Niccolo, looked at him strangely.

Massimo ignored him and walked to the stairway. As he labored up the steep steps he thought of his friend, Renato. Lorenzo's father was in mourning. Ever since the gravely wounded duke had returned, escorted by the battered remnants of his personal guard, signor Arrighi feared that his son, if not already dead, was probably lost to him forever. And as each day passed with no news of the boy, the father's grief deepened. The last two days he had not left his studio, even for meals. Although Renato's suffering only deepened his own sorrow, Massimo had decided he would "hope" for both of them. Perhaps that was the voice that urged him to visit the roof one more time.

Many times as a soldier Massimo's superior eyesight had proved to be immensely valuable. It was his sighting of the Florentine column that had saved the duke from certain ambush. Now, as he scanned the southern horizon, he searched for any sign that would give his old friend some reason to hope.

He focused on the road. Summer always brought more travelers: farmers and merchants from other parts of Italy, even religious pilgrims on their way to shrines to pray for favors. Lately there had been an increase in travelers from the south. People were fleeing the ravages of the mercenaries. Cheated of the loot they expected, the mercenaries had taken to robbing the local peasants and tradesmen. For some reason, however, they spared monks and nuns. That was why Massimo looked especially hard for anyone wearing a religious habit. They might have some news.

Ten minutes, then twice that, passed; nothing unusual appeared. Massimo, once again despairing of his efforts, was about to leave the tower when he spotted a lone brown-robed figure. He was coming from the south, walking, it seemed, with unusual determination. Massimo squinted to get a little more detail. And for the first time in all these hours and days of futility, his heart skipped and he wanted to cry with joy. Hanging from the monk's shoulder was a leather travel case; even at this distance he recognized it as the one he had made for Lorenzo on the boy's twelfth birthday.

His bad leg forgotten, Massimo flew down the stairs. Within seconds Niccolo had been sent on horseback to fetch the monk to the armory. Massimo's instructions to his apprentice had been simple: "Bring him back here, or don't come back at all."

Of course, the master armorer had no reason to know that at that very moment the good brother Ambrose was at the south gate inquiring as to the whereabouts of the Arrighi armory.

Chapter 28

The first two hundred paces were sheer agony for the boy. If he had been with anyone other than Beatrice, he would have fainted or fallen long before going that far. But Lorenzo would have died before disgracing himself in front of Beatrice.

"How far did they say the inn was?" He measured his words carefully so as not to reveal the difficulty he was having with his breathing. The wound may have looked better, but something inside was so bruised that any movement was an effort. *How, Lord, am I going to ride Scoppio once I get him?* he asked himself. He turned to look at Beatrice's family. Their courage was remarkable. He could bear his pain.

The lepers were always careful to stay a certain distance from him, just as they had in the small camp where he'd recuperated. It had been especially hard for Beatrice's family to keep away because of the gratitude they felt toward him for rescuing their daughter. But they had found a way to thank him. They had discovered where the mercenaries were staying. It seemed that foreigners, too, needed a place to recover from wounds.

"The inn is about five miles from here, just outside Siena's walls. Pilgrims told my mother that the German soldiers have taken over. They have driven away the guests and are terrorizing the innkeeper and his wife." Beatrice spoke without looking at Lorenzo. She didn't want him to see her concern. She'd wanted more rest for him, but once he'd heard about Scoppio there had been no stopping him.

The small party stayed within the cover of the woods. Even though everyone avoided lepers, Lorenzo wanted to keep their presence hidden. He couldn't take the chance that some roaming band of mercenaries would see him or Beatrice and alert Scoppio's captors.

Lorenzo had thought long and hard about the best way of rescuing Scoppio. Force was out of the question. His only hope was to immobilize the mercenaries long enough to free his horse and escape. But he was certain that sooner or later the young mercenary, the one obsessed with Scoppio, would follow them. And Lorenzo knew that he and his warhorse would never be free of the youth until they were within their city's walls—or he was dead. Finally he shared his concerns with Beatrice, and together they devised a plan that they hoped would give him enough time to get far away.

By late that afternoon they had reached the vicinity of

the inn. Lorenzo went ahead to scout around; it was possible the foreigners had left. When he was within a hundred paces of the inn he saw something curious: a hastily constructed enclosure that contained about two dozen horses. *So that is their plan—steal as many horses as possible, then sell them.* The thought at first gave him doubts about their own plan, but then he saw it as an opportunity.

Suddenly the horses, who had been grazing quietly, ran to the corner of the corral. When Lorenzo saw the reason, he almost shouted with relief. Scoppio had stormed out of the stables. The warhorse was safe and as healthy as ever. The boy started toward the woods, and he turned to look at his horse. *I'll be back tonight, Scoppio,* he promised. *I will not lose you again.*

Chapter 29

In midsummer, twilight is long and slow to turn to night. Beatrice and Lorenzo needed darkness for their plan to be a success; it would create confusion among the mercenaries at the inn and give Lorenzo cover for his escape. So, the two had to wait until nightfall—and a sign from the innkeeper that the plan was working.

Earlier that afternoon Beatrice, dressed as an old farm woman, had visited the inn. She told the innkeepers that this was their chance to flee and gave them the poisonous mushrooms Lorenzo had picked. When the soldiers fell sick with violent cramps and weakness, Lorenzo would rescue Scoppio and scatter the mercenaries' horses, and the innkeepers could escape to Siena and safety. The two frightened souls had not needed convincing. They had been brutalized and knew it was only a matter of time before the mercenaries killed them as they had so many others.

"What are you thinking, Lorenzo? Can you tell me?"

The best of the boletus — delicious!

A pure white amanita — deadly!

Beatrice and Lorenzo were sitting next to each other at the base of an old stone cistern. Lorenzo noted its masonry, its Roman origin. The ruins of that ancient empire had always fascinated him.

But it wasn't Roman ruins that were in his thoughts and his heart this evening; it was Beatrice. Until he'd met her, his future had been in his hands. It was he, even against his father's wishes, who had decided to be a knight; he had trained Scoppio to be a warhorse. Even his ability to draw, which he accepted as others would the air they breathed, had been put to the service of that goal. Then came the battle and the storm, the lepers, and then Beatrice.

"You are worried about getting back to your city through the roaming bands of foreigners, aren't you, Lorenzo?" The young woman sounded concerned. It was a very real threat that the boy faced.

Lorenzo turned so that he could see her. He was smiling. "I am thinking of Massimo's laughter when I tell him that his mushrooms were my strongest weapon against the Germans."

Beatrice laughed. Lorenzo was surprised and pleased—he had never heard her laugh before. But he wasn't pleased with his answer, for it had been a lie. He had been afraid to say what was really on his mind. He could not tell her that he dreaded never seeing her again.

The sky was darkening; candles had already been lit at the inn. The mercenaries were probably getting ready to eat. When the signal came, the time for talk would end. He would have to leave immediately; the lepers and Beatrice, too, would have to get as far from this place as possible. If he were ever going to tell her what was in his heart, it had to be now. The boy sighed deeply. He turned toward her.

"Beatrice . . . this afternoon, when you were at the inn, your mother spoke to me. What she said—what she wished for you—were words I wanted to say, but dared not." Lorenzo paused. He searched for the right words. "Beatrice, you have changed my life. Before I met you, I . . . I thought I knew what was important. Now everything seems empty and vain . . . and I don't know why." Lorenzo was standing.

The last light of dusk outlined his body, shimmering slightly over his boots and dagger.

Beatrice listened, her eyes lowered, her lips slightly open. Lorenzo could see she was struggling to control her emotions. He reached out to her; she took his hand and pulled herself up.

The young woman, her hand still in his, took his other hand and held them both tightly. "Lorenzo, I know my mother loves me deeply. As I know your father, and Massimo, love you."

The boy was embarrassed and surprised by her last words. "Yes, I know my father and Massimo love me; they'd do anything for me. They'd even give their lives for me." His own words surprised him, but he knew they were true.

"Their love is without question, without demands. They value your life more than their own, as my mother values mine over hers." Beatrice looked at him, hoping for his understanding.

Lorenzo's heart was pounding. He couldn't speak.

"Lorenzo . . . I have been blessed. I am free of the horrible sickness that has cursed my family. That is God's gift to me. If I know that my parents would give their lives for me, can I not share my gift with them?"

Lorenzo heard the simple honesty of her voice. There was nothing he could answer. Would he not do the same? Could he not share a gift from God with those he loved? But what was his gift? What had God given him to share with others?

Beatrice was still holding his hands. She lowered them so that the palms faced up. "You have beautiful hands, Lorenzo . . . and gifted." She looked up at him, her eyes searching his. "I have seen your work—in your satchel that Brother Ambrose is taking to your father. Before my parents' leprosy was discovered and we were driven from our city, I saw many such fine drawings. But none as beautiful as . . ." Beatrice had reached the limits of her self-control. She broke into sobs, put her hands to her face and turned away from Lorenzo.

The boy stood motionless, silent. He was powerless.

The two remained that way for what felt to Lorenzo like his entire life. He was aware of nothing else. Time did not pass, the sky stayed the same deep dark blue, the air did not move; they were surrounded by sorrow. But Lorenzo could not bear the finality of her words. *There must be some way,* he thought. *There must be.*

"Beatrice." His voice was but the slightest of whispers. "Let me take all of you back with me. My father and the duke will see to it that your family is cared for; you will not be abandoning them, I promise you."

The young woman remained silent. After a while she dropped her hands from her face and looked at him. In the days and weeks ahead, when he was tempted to come back and search for her in hopes of changing her mind, he would remember the resignation in her eyes.

"Lorenzo, when Brother Ambrose returns your drawings to your father, he will tell him that you were saved and cared for by peasants driven from their land by the mercenaries. No one will ever know you lived among lepers. Lorenzo, you *must* promise me—" she took his face in her hands, tears filled her eyes, her lips trembled "—you must never tell anyone about me or my family." Her weeping had rendered the last words almost inaudible.

She held his face for a few seconds, then slowly let her hands fall to her sides. Her sorrow was almost too painful for Lorenzo.

Gradually Beatrice recovered. She took a cloth from the folds of her dress and gently wiped Lorenzo's face. He had been so concerned with her, he'd barely noticed his own tears. Embarrassed, he turned toward the inn. Nothing was happening. It suddenly occurred to him that the plan might fail and he would have to remain with Beatrice for a bit longer. It was not an unwelcome thought.

Beatrice took Lorenzo's hand. "Soon, Lorenzo, the innkeeper will signal you that the plan is working." Beatrice was calmer now. Her voice was soft but insistent. "You must get Scoppio and ride out of here as quickly as you can." She handed him a small bundle of provisions she had packed for his journey.

The boy slung the parcel over his shoulder, then impulsively took Beatrice's hands into his. "Are you sure, Beatrice? Is there really no hope?"

The young woman's eyes were dark with fear. "Lorenzo, I pray you never see the loathing I've seen in the faces of strangers. If people knew you had been among us, they would mark you as a leper—forever. I would never let that happen to you, Lorenzo, *never!*" She pressed her hands against his, then tore free and ran into the darkness of the woods.

He wanted to follow her, but something from the direction of the inn caught his eye. It was a lantern, swinging— the signal.

With a cry of anger and despair he grabbed the pointed wooden staves he had made and ran across the darkened patch of meadow that separated the woods from the inn. The two innkeepers were waiting by the horses, eager to tell him that the hated mercenaries were getting what they deserved. In the darkness they could not see the tears that ran down his face.

A familiar sound greeted him as he undid the crude gate. Scoppio nuzzled him so hard he nearly fell over. Quickly he got horses for the couple, helped them mount, and sent them on their way. He climbed onto Scoppio and herded the rest of the horses through the gate to freedom. *That should slow down the mercenaries,* he thought, *if they ever recover from Massimo's mushrooms.*

He had tried not to think of Beatrice, but the remembrance of his jest about mushrooms brought back the sound of her laughter, and all of the sadness that followed. The grief he'd put aside reappeared; sorrow filled his heart.

I must think only of getting away, he reminded himself, but as he turned his horse toward home, his heart felt darker than the night.

Chapter 30

When his housekeeper had delayed his departure in order to prepare extra provisions, signor Arrighi had been annoyed; he was desperate to get on the road to find his son. Now that the search had already consumed four days of a journey that should have taken half the time, he was glad she had been so insistent. Massimo agreed.

The two men were nearing exhaustion. They had been in the saddle almost constantly since Brother Ambrose had given them the good news that Lorenzo was alive. To make matters more difficult, there was no inn they dared visit. The duke's patrols protected travelers close to their city. But beyond that, it was a no-man's-land. Terror hid around every turn in the road. Bands of foreign mercenaries roamed freely, robbing and burning at will. After the rout of his army, Count Barzio decided he need not pay the mercenaries. In retaliation, the foreign soldiers were making the count's peasants pay dearly.

On this, the fifth day, both men were determined to reach the area the monk had described as being the place he'd last seen Lorenzo. From there they hoped to pick up the boy's trail.

"It promises to be very hot today, Renato." Massimo had just finished his breakfast of cheese and bread and was saddling his mount. His friend, already on his horse, agreed and wondered aloud whether they should continue wearing the light armor Massimo had insisted on.

"Old friend, the minute we shed our armor, mercenaries will appear out of nowhere, armed to the teeth." Massimo had gotten on his horse. He checked the lead to the extra horse they had brought for Lorenzo and started toward a clearing they had noticed the night before. The monk had mentioned such a place, and this seemed to be in the right direction.

"Massimo," signor Arrighi began, "I confess I am getting discouraged. I had hoped we would have seen some sign of Lorenzo, or at least travelers who had seen him or the horse, but . . ." His voice trailed off and he lowered his head.

Massimo's heart was heavy. He hated to see his old friend quit, not now when they could be so close. He could still hear the cry of relief Renato had uttered when the monk placed the boy's satchel of drawings in his hands. Of course the father had been concerned when he heard of Lorenzo's wound, but the monk's reassurances had calmed his fears.

"Come on, old friend. Don't give up. You shall have your son back, and I predict it will happen today." Massimo was doing his best to keep his friend's spirits up and it was working.

"Do you wish to name the hour, Massimo?" Signor Arrighi was sitting up straight in the saddle again.

"Of course." He squinted into the rising sun. It had just come up and its rays were nearly horizontal, almost blinding them. "Before the sun has traveled a quarter of its journey, we—you and me and Lorenzo—shall be on our way home to the biggest celebration the house of Arrighi has ever seen." Massimo was shading his eyes. He could barely make out the clearing that lay ahead of them.

"I pray you are right. I shall outdo the duke himself." At the mention of the duke, Lorenzo's father stopped. When he continued, his voice was more serious. "I have been thinking about the duke's request. I am not sure I can agree to . . ."

A flock of mourning doves shot out of the trees about fifty paces in front of them. Massimo's soldier's instincts quickly took command. "Wait, Renato—we have company up ahead."

Both men strained to see into the woods, but the sun kept blurring their vision. They actually heard the soldiers charge before they saw them.

Chapter 31

The musty odor of the forest floor was Lorenzo's first sensation when he awoke early on the second morning after his flight from the mercenaries. The second feeling was a crushing sense of loss.

Beatrice was a world away now. She had refused his offer of help—to save him from the curse of leprosy. Painfully he raised himself, first to a sitting position, then to his feet. He had fallen asleep from exhaustion; the better part of two nights and a day had been spent avoiding small groups of foreign soldiers intent on killing and looting. His situation was dangerous, and he had begun to question his chances of escape, but the danger was far less oppressive than the sorrow.

He led Scoppio to a small brook he had crossed earlier. "Drink now, boy. It's going to be hot today." Lorenzo passed his hand over the horse. That had been a surprise—the horse's condition. When Lorenzo had last seen Scoppio he'd been covered with mud, pinned beneath a dead animal, and surrounded by the ghastly remains of battle. Yet the horse never looked better. He had been right about the young German's obsession; Scoppio was more than a mere spoil of war to the mercenary. *How odd,* he thought. *He's tried to kill me twice, but he loves this creature as much as I do.*

Lorenzo pulled himself up on Scoppio. The magnificent warhorse, used to wearing the finest trappings, looked little better than a tinker's mule. His flanks were festooned with straps fashioned from anything Lorenzo could find. All the boy's belongings—the spears, Beatrice's parcel, the duke's helmet—hung from them, the result of his escaping without a saddle. Lorenzo patted his horse reassuringly. "You may look like a peddler's pony, Scoppio, but you are still the best horse in Italy."

The boy lay his head alongside the animal's neck and inhaled deeply. The smell of a horse; why was it so comforting? He'd had the horse since he was a colt, a present from his father on his seventh birthday. His mother had died a few months earlier and all he'd felt was an absence, a cold emptiness. It had been a mystery to him, but very real and frightening.

The horse had been his father's attempt to get him out of his grief, to get him laughing and playing again. And it had worked. He and Scoppio had grown up together, just like brothers. They had learned all about knights and warhorses, and later, when Massimo got involved, about armor, about tactics of war, about honor and chivalry.

Lorenzo slowly sat upright, reluctant to leave memories of a time that seemed so simple, so clear. He knew more now—too much more.

The horse had been walking east. Lorenzo hoped to go around the heaviest concentration of marauders. Then he would swing north past the site of the battle and, he prayed, reach the city by dark. Ahead of him was a large open area. He decided to keep to the cover of the woods. He stayed north of the clearing, still going east.

Suddenly he was blinded. The sun had just risen and was shining directly into his eyes. He almost laughed aloud at how things, large and small, kept getting in his way. Then he remembered the duke's helmet. He reached around and unfastened it. He put it on; fortunately the cool of the morning kept it from being suffocating, and it worked.

"Much better, boy. Now I can see where we're going." Lorenzo dug his heels into the horse's flanks and the big animal responded. "Let's see if we can cover some ground, hey, Scoppio? You're probably dreaming about those buckets of grain I used to feed you, right?" Talking to his horse was a habit Lorenzo had begun as a small boy; it always made him feel better.

The forest was more open here, the trees farther apart and the ground flat and free of debris. The view through his visor was clear but restricted. He raised it to get a wider picture of his surroundings. What he saw sent a chill through his body. Mercenaries, three of them, waiting for something, or someone.

He looked to his left. There were two men on horse-back, leading a third horse, probably merchants, and most likely unaware of the danger that was ahead. *Oh, God, in another minute this madness will cause two more senseless deaths.* The thought infuriated him. "We can't let this happen, can we, boy?" he whispered to his horse as he quickly undid the wooden staves. He moved to his left so as to be able to interrupt the mercenaries' charge. The travel-ers must at least have swords, he reasoned. His actions would give them time to react.

A flock of mourning doves exploded into the air; the soldiers were charging. Lorenzo was ready. "All right, Scoppio, let's show them a real warhorse!" He snapped his visor shut and jabbed his heels hard. The horse exploded into action.

Chapter 32

Lorenzo's father was directly in the path of the soldiers; and one of them, holding a lance, was charging straight at him. The master armorer had seen enough jousts and battles to know that he was about to die. But he drew his sword in the fragile hope of parrying the lance. The soldier was only fifty paces away. Renato had no time to turn and run, just time enough to commend his soul to God and hope that He, in His infinite mercy, would grant a father's final wish: that Lorenzo, wherever he was, be spared.

Ready for death, he looked to his left. Massimo, his old friend, was in the same desperate situation, only he faced two men. One had his sword out and the other wielded a deadly spiked ball. He shuddered. Massimo had pulled the extra horse up to his side, hoping to put an obstacle in their paths.

Suddenly Renato Arrighi, master armorer, head of the house of Arrighi, stood in his stirrups and, in a final burst of courage, raised his sword and shouted to his friend, "Massimo, together—we go to meet Death!"

At that very instant a white stallion flashed by the armorer's right side and headed for the charging soldier.

There was a split second when all but the rider and his white horse seemed to stop in midstride. It passed so quickly that years later none of the participants could swear that it really happened. But the result, whatever the cause, was not in dispute. The enemy in that moment lost their advantage.

Their first casualty was the charging soldier. Signor Arrighi, who seconds earlier had faced certain death, watched in stunned disbelief as an armored rider with a lance was unhorsed by a boy with a stave. Afterward he would remember the sound of the splintering stick against the mercenary's breastplate and the sight of the enemy soldier being hurled backward in a low arc that ended with a crunching thud amid a cloud of earth and leaves.

But Lorenzo's father was still in jeopardy. With Massimo going blade to blade with one soldier, the other turned toward Renato, his spiked ball flailing murderously above his head. Lorenzo's father brandished his sword hoping to catch the spinning chain and disarm the mercenary. The soldier swung the ball. Its chain wrapped around the sword blade; the soldier pulled, yanking the sword out of Renato's hand.

Signor Arrighi, for the second time in less than a minute, found himself face-to-face with death. The soldier had only to untangle the sword from his weapon. Renato, defenseless and exhausted, waited for the inevitable.

"Father! Father! Quick, get on Scoppio!" The boy swooped alongside his father's horse and pulled him onto the warhorse. The maneuver caught friend and foe off guard. Renato couldn't believe his eyes. Lorenzo was here! His son *was* alive!

Renato's and the extra horse ran off. The two remaining mercenaries quickly broke off fighting and chased after the two horses. Not taking any chances, Massimo, followed by Lorenzo and his father on Scoppio, turned and rode north. Lorenzo, who was having trouble getting a good seat behind his father, fell behind Massimo.

Two hands suddenly reached up and grabbed hold of the leather straps that held Renato's empty scabbard. "Lorenzo!" he cried out.

Lorenzo looked down. The mercenary he had unhorsed, the one who had stolen Scoppio, was pulling on the straps, determined to drag his father from the horse. Lorenzo yelled at the youth to let go, but his words were useless. He dug his heels into Scoppio, urging him on, hoping to loosen the soldier's hold. But the youth held on, unyielding in his effort to drag Renato from the horse. Renato tried to wrest the strap from the attacker's grip, but he had no strength left. Desperate, he cried out, "Lorenzo! Your knife. Cut the strap, hurry!"

His son pulled his dagger and began slicing at the strap.

When he saw the dagger the mercenary became frantic. In one final effort he pulled himself up and grabbed for

Renato's throat. At that same moment Lorenzo sliced down on the strap. The blade slid along the shiny leather and collided with the lunging soldier. The tip slipped over the rim of the youth's breastplate and plunged deep into his neck.

Lorenzo's father, twisted and bent over by the soldier's weight, saw the blood gush from the wound, splattering over Lorenzo's hand. He saw the horror and shock in the soldier's face mirrored in the eyes of his son.

Unwilling to lose what he valued more than his life, the dying mercenary clung to the leather strap until his eyes glazed over and his body hung lifeless against the shoulder of the horse.

Massimo had turned back when he realized his companions had fallen behind. Renato and his son dismounted. The three stood over the dead soldier. The other mercenaries had fled with their loot and their wounds. The forest was peaceful again. The birds had returned.

Signor Arrighi embraced his son. "God has answered my prayers, Lorenzo; you are safe." He turned to Massimo. "You were right, my old friend. The sun is barely halfway to its zenith and we are about to return home."

The two men watched as Lorenzo knelt beside the dead youth. The mercenary, signor Arrighi realized, was not much older than his own son.

"I want to bury him, Father," Lorenzo said. He looked at both men.

For a few seconds no one said anything. Finally his father broke the silence.

"Lorenzo, so much has happened in the last few minutes that I can barely make sense of it; there must be much you have to tell us, but I have one question now." Signor Arrighi paused, looking down at the fallen mercenary. "Is there a special reason you are honoring this enemy? He tried to kill us, yet you give him this respect."

Lorenzo, still on his knees, looked up at his father and godfather. "He tried to kill me twice before, but he loved Scoppio and treated him very well. For that reason I will save his body from being torn apart by wild animals."

The two men looked at each other. The older Arrighi nodded and all three began digging a shallow grave.

Lorenzo gathered some stones to mark the spot and with the others' help, put the slain enemy in his grave.

The three men and two horses began their return to their city. They all were exhausted, almost too weak to talk. But Massimo did make a remark that brought a rare smile to the tired boy's features.

"During the sword fight, I could barely hold my own. Any soldier should have been able to overcome me. But the one I was fighting seemed even weaker. I wondered why?"

"You are smiling, son. Is there a reason?" his father asked. Lorenzo nodded, but said nothing. The smile gradually faded; he turned away so the others could not see his tears.

Chapter 33

The sky was bluer than he had seen in a long time. Big, blossoming white clouds floated majestically across the heavens like a Venetian armada setting out to sea. He had seen sailing ships but once in his life and had never ceased wondering about them and the distant worlds they visited. He wished he could be far away, anywhere but here. Heavyhearted and confused, Lorenzo sought comfort and answers here on the tower every day since his return.

The last three days had been painfully unreal to him. A joyful celebration of his return that had begun with a mixture of laughter and tears had ended with the most wrenching conversation he'd ever had with his father. He thanked God that Massimo had been present to help both of them through it.

But even his godfather's sympathy and wisdom were not enough to bridge the gap that separated him from his father. The boy knew he was asking a lot of his father. How could his father understand him? How could anyone? Beatrice's warnings and his promise never to speak of the lepers were a burden. His vow of secrecy extended to all, even his father and Massimo. And if they couldn't know about Beatrice and what she had meant to him, they would never be able to understand anything.

Now he was facing the biggest decision of his life.

"Lorenzo, your horse is ready." Roberto spoke from the top step of the stairwell.

"Did you use my war saddle and trappings?" Lorenzo asked.

"Yes, but I left off the armor; it is very warm," Roberto answered.

Lorenzo nodded in agreement. "I'll be down soon. Tell my father and Massimo that I will be going to the palace alone." He looked again at the long view of the valley that ran south from the city. Somewhere in that war-torn countryside, Beatrice and her family were on their endless journey, a journey with no earthly destination, sustained by nothing more than a daughter's love and devotion. His heart ached.

On the horizon a green haze was all he could see of the distant forest; the resting place of the mercenary he'd killed. He looked down at his hand. Even at this distance in space and time he could see and feel the blood as it splattered violently over his hand and arm; he could still see the expression in the young soldier's eyes—the shock and horror that reflected his own. In some mysterious way his love for Beatrice and his grief over the soldier were connected. They were part of him, and would be forever.

"The duke is waiting, Lorenzo. Hurry." Roberto's voice echoed up the stairs.

A large cloud covered the sun; a shadow fell over the tower. Lorenzo turned and descended the stairs.

The crowd appeared as soon as he crossed the piazza in front of the cathedral. First it followed him at a distance. Then as more people arrived, it came closer. Then it began shouting, "Long live Lorenzo!"

He sat straight up in the saddle in spite of the pain that still lingered in his back. He tried to look only to the front, to concentrate on the right words to use when he spoke to the duke. From the reaction of the people it was plain to see what everyone, including the duke, expected. And his father, after much pressure from Massimo, had agreed to leave the final decision to his son.

He and Scoppio were only minutes from the palace. He dared not look back, but from the noise and the fervor of the chants, he guessed that the crowd was still growing. This, he realized, is what the future would look and sound like to a ruler. Every public occasion—an official betrothal to the daughter of some important ally, their wedding, the baptism of each child, wars, deaths—any event or decision that affected the city and its people was an enormous responsibility. He completely understood why the duke needed an heir.

Fifty paces from the palace steps a young boy on a

spirited black charger rode up alongside Scoppio. The two stallions eyed each other suspiciously, Scoppio tossing his head and snorting.

"Your permission, sire, to speak." The boy, younger than Lorenzo, waited respectfully, his hand over his heart in a sign of loyalty.

My Lord, Lorenzo thought. *They have anointed me already.* He nodded, then added, "You have a beautiful horse. Did you train him yourself?"

"Yes, sire, and . . ." The boy was suddenly embarrassed at his own boldness.

"Go on." Lorenzo smiled, not at the boy's awkwardness, but at the remembrance of his own.

"I have come to pledge my loyalty to you. I am young, but my horse and I look forward to the day when we will have the honor of serving you and our great city." The boy saluted again with a slight bow and was about to ride away when Lorenzo signaled him to wait.

Lorenzo reached to his waist and removed his dagger. Holding it in his hand, he waved the boy closer. "Your duke and his city are pleased by your oath. Take this as a sign of their gratitude."

Lorenzo continued to the palace. He could well imagine the boy's sense of exhilaration.

As soon as he reached the foot of the palace steps two of the duke's aides came to his side. Lorenzo dismounted. One of them took hold of Scoppio's bridle to lead him away. The horse turned to Lorenzo. He tossed his head, shaking his mane. He gave a low whinny, then with a final snort of annoyance, went with the aide.

Lorenzo climbed the broad marble steps of the palace. He turned toward the square, which was filled to overflowing. The crowd following him had tripled in size and had been joined by others, all eager to witness the duke's first public appearance with his newly adopted son and heir.

Lorenzo stood there, transfixed by the enormity of this occasion. The crowd, seeing him pause, seized the moment. He was their hero. He had saved the duke once, then, with his return of the duke's horse, had salvaged the duke's honor and their city's. No son, no future ruler could have done more to deserve their praise. Their cheers rose in a crescendo that shook Lorenzo to his roots. He stepped forward and with a deep bow acknowledged their love, and prayed in his heart for their understanding.

He turned. The commander of the palace guard smiled approvingly, then led him into the palace.

Lorenzo heard the heavy doors close behind him, muffling the noise of the crowd. The soldier led him down a corridor to a room he had never seen. The door was open. The commander of the guard stepped aside respectfully.

"The duke is waiting, Lorenzo."

Chapter 34

He was alone now, except for the duke.

The duke sat behind a large table. There were documents laid out before him, and one end was set with an assortment of glassware and wine decanters. There were also small platters of delicacies and settings enough for several people. It was obvious that a modest and private celebration had been anticipated for Lorenzo's family and the duke's closest advisers.

The duke sat in the large chair he used whenever he was considering important affairs of state such as this one. He was wearing his best tunic, one that fit loosely over the heavily bandaged upper portion of his body—proof, Lorenzo realized, of the duke's close brush with death at hands of the mercenaries.

As Lorenzo walked across the long room he became aware of the large murals that decorated the entire chamber. Scenes representing the history of the duke's family and the city circled the room. Behind the duke a painting in three panels celebrated a great victory over the Florentines. The middle and largest panel portrayed the battle's decisive moment and featured the duke's grandfather astride a magnificent warhorse, white, exactly like Scoppio.

The two side panels were filled with portraits of family members and important citizens. He could see where new faces had been added over time. His artist's imagination readily pictured the duke's face beside his own, gazing together with pride at their ancestor's accomplishment.

The vision made clear to him the immense importance of the decision he was about to make. As he approached the duke, who was patiently waiting to greet him, two more faces from his imagination took their places on the mural.

Beneath the hooves of the triumphant stallion in the painting lay a fallen enemy. His helmet was missing, blood flowed discreetly from a wound to his throat, and his eyes, as blue as those of the slain mercenary, stared upward in total disbelief at his fate.

To the right and just behind his own imagined portrait, a young woman of beatific beauty and sadness looked aside, alone in her rejection of the violence.

"Welcome, Lorenzo." The duke's warm smile momentarily erased the lines of pain that threatened to become a permanent feature of his face. "I see you are enjoying a look into the history of our proud city and my—or should I say *our* noble family."

"Yes, sire. The paintings are alive, and I see now why Scoppio was destined to belong to you. He is back in your stables, my lord, and looking better than ever." Lorenzo was relieved that he could begin his meeting on this pleasant note.

At the mention of the horse the duke touched his left shoulder, the twinge of pain barely registering on the ruler's face. "Your gift, my boy, saved my life—again. You've heard how he charged and reared and fought off my attackers. If it had not been for the rain . . ." The duke stopped, anger swept over his face, then receded. "It is good to see you, Lorenzo. Your father and I feared the worst. I only wish I could reward the peasants who saved you, but I am told that is not possible. Someday I will find a way to express my gratitude for your survival."

The duke was tired; it was obvious to Lorenzo that his wounds had weakened him. He was leaning back in his chair, waiting for Lorenzo to speak, waiting for an answer to a request he'd first made to the boy's father just before going to war against Count Barzio.

Lorenzo could not keep the duke waiting a moment longer. "My lord, Your Excellency, I and my father and his father before him, five generations of Arrighis, have been proud to serve the noble goals of your family—" the boy looked around at the murals "—as you fought and died for our beloved and magnificent city. To be part of your achievements, to have shared, however humbly, in your victories has been all the reward we sought. But your generosity to the house of Arrighi has been . . ." Lorenzo stopped to contain his emotions. He saw the duke studying him, an expression of concern and kindness softening his hawklike gaze.

The boy continued, "Your generosity to our house, to me, has become legendary. And now to add this honor, to want this, your humblest of servants, to be part of—" Lorenzo swept his hand around the room "—this majestic heritage is . . . is an act of love that has moved my father and me beyond any feelings we could ever have imagined."

The boy stopped and reached into the leather satchel that hung from his shoulder. He pulled out a sheaf of drawings and spread them before his puzzled listener. He had come to the end of his answer; he knew his words would be unworthy of his feelings. He wanted the duke to look into his soul, to see what he himself had discovered in the aftermath of that horrendous battle.

The duke rose heavily from his chair. With one hand on the table for support, he went through the sepia drawings one by one. Lorenzo watched the expression on the ruler's face, looking for the right moment to say what had to be said.

"Lorenzo, my boy, I have always known you had a gift, but these drawings go beyond anything I've seen, from your hand or—" the duke lifted his head to look at the panels surrounding him "—even in these."

Lorenzo flushed with embarrassment. "My lord, you honor me—"

He was cut off by the duke, who continued as if he had not heard the boy. "I have been in many battles, my son, and seen too many horrors, but never before have I felt the tragedy of war as I do now." He picked up a drawing of a dead soldier, his helmet gone, his eyes staring into those of the viewer. He was young, handsome, and had the look of a warrior; his armor revealed him as an enemy. "He is young, so young," the duke continued, "and he looks like he was brave. He would have become an excellent comrade. . . ." The duke put the drawing down and covered his face with both hands.

Lorenzo saw his shoulders sag forward ever so slightly. The duke, Lorenzo realized, was mourning his own son, killed at a very young age in a skirmish just outside the city walls.

The duke had regained control. One drawing remained. It, like the dead soldier, was a portrait—of a young woman. Her face, her slightly sad smile, attracted the duke, compelling him to look deeply into the sepia tones that formed the soulful eyes that asked unanswerable questions. "Who is she?" the duke asked, fully convinced that the picture was the likeness of someone real.

Lorenzo yearned to tell the duke all about Beatrice. He desperately wanted to tell him about this wonderful person who had forced him to face the truth about his dream, this young woman whose beauty was too subtle for his talent. He wanted to tell her story, to see the words come alive in another's face as he told of her selfless love and unbelievable courage. But his vow silenced the truth. "One of the peasant girls, my lord, who attended me when I was wounded. I . . . I didn't know her name."

The duke studied the picture for a few minutes more, then put it down next to the other drawings. When he looked up at Lorenzo his expression had changed. He walked slowly around the table to where the boy was standing.

"My son, and I call you that from my heart, I can see clearly that your future is not what either of us thought it would be." The duke took the boy's hands in his; he looked at the room full of paintings, then turned back to the boy. "Lorenzo, when I saw the drawings you did for my armor, I said to myself, the boy draws like an angel. When I saw the drawing of the young woman, I said to myself, the boy has seen an angel—and has captured her—for all to see. That, my son, is a gift, a gift far more rare than that of a warrior. Therefore, as your sovereign, as the person you must obey, I release you from any vow you made to serve me on the field of battle. I desire only that you use your gift for the glory of our city and of God." The duke embraced Lorenzo, then ordered a servant to send for Lorenzo's father and godfather. There would be a celebration after all.

Lorenzo began to gather his drawings. As he put each one away he remembered his thoughts being so confused, so dark, that his only hope had been to pour out his story in the drawings.

He looked at the picture of Beatrice. He had worked by candlelight to finish it. Every detail had been lovingly

A fallen soldier

brought to life, the golden light around her curls, the dark
eyes, the rich, embroidered bodice that framed the delicate
curve of her neck and shoulders. It was not the dress of a
peasant. He smiled. His art had betrayed him. Had the duke
noticed the fabric of Beatrice's dress? Lorenzo knew it didn't
matter. He knew that the duke would never ask, would

never pry into his soul. The duke had once again proved to be a man worthy of his loyalty. Now he would have the rest of his life to prove himself worthy of the duke's trust and Beatrice's love.

EPILOGUE
Twenty years later

"Brother, come down, please. We have visitors." The young monk's voice echoed through the vaulted chamber.

The artist lay on his back on the scaffold. He worked quickly. Once the wet plaster had been applied to the wall, the color had to be added before it set. The monk painted confidently, modeling the flowing robes that covered the kneeling figure of Saint Joseph. Although it was summer, the beads of sweat that formed on the painter's brow were not caused by the warmth. They were the result of pain.

Lorenzo worked through the pain, intent on finishing this section before the light deteriorated. He had already completed most of the church. Only the interior of the dome remained. But much of that had to be done lying down, and that meant more pain.

"These are special visitors, Brother," the monk called out again.

"I'm sorry, Brother, I can't leave now. The light will be gone soon and I still have much—" Lorenzo was interrupted.

"You ordered me to get you immediately—no matter what you were doing—whenever they came to our door." The monk was respectful, but insistent.

Lorenzo slowly rose to a kneeling position. He gathered his brushes and tools and began his descent from the platform. Hand over hand he carefully climbed down the rickety ladder that made up one end of the scaffold. "How many are there, Brother?" he asked.

The young monk hesitated, then spoke. "There are three, no, there are four—but only three of them appear to be afflicted with . . ."

"Leprosy. It's all right to speak that word, Brother." Lorenzo had reached the church floor. "I know how much terror the word holds for you, but believe me—they may be outcasts to men, but to God they are as precious as you or I, maybe more so." Lorenzo began walking out to the courtyard. "Now, what were you saying about three and four?"

"Well, there are . . . three lepers, and two of them are carrying a fourth, a woman. She seems to be very ill, but not with leprosy."

Lorenzo stopped so suddenly that the younger monk nearly walked into him. "The woman, the one who is ill but not with leprosy—is she old, very old?"

The monk shook his head, "No . . . she is . . . of course

she is ill and thin, but she is about your age, perhaps a bit older. And . . ."

"Yes, go on, what were you going to say?" Lorenzo impatiently prodded the young man.

"I was struck by her beauty, Brother. It has a quality that . . ."

Lorenzo left the young monk in midsentence. He'd heard enough.

He crossed the courtyard deliberately, afraid of confirming what he already knew. Each large paving stone, as it slipped beneath his sandals, seemed to mark a year in his life. And the closer he came to the cloister door and what lay beyond it, the clearer the past became.

His father, God rest his soul, dead for many years; Massimo, his godfather, teacher, protector, unable to walk, but thank the Lord, still alive, still helping the apprentices who had continued the armory; and the duke, never again the power he had once been, but still clever enough to bring his city into an alliance with Siena, and generous enough to build this church. Every day these last ten years he'd prayed for the duke's soul, as he had for the young soldier he'd killed so many years ago.

He reached the door, the thick wooden door that some of his brothers imagined could keep out the world and all its sorrows. He looked back at the courtyard he had just crossed. The young monk was still there, watching, sensing perhaps that something significant was about to happen.

Lorenzo's gaze moved past the monk, past the church,

past the monastery roof to the green fields beyond. He smiled. A boy was riding a horse across the crest of a hill. The horse was white, but not as large as Scoppio or, he imagined, as strong or courageous. His beloved warhorse was gone too. But, he remembered gratefully, Scoppio never had to put on armor and fight again. It had been the duke's wish.

Lorenzo stood on the stone threshold and pulled on the wrought-iron handle. The huge door swung open. The lepers stood there waiting patiently, as they had waited at so many gates so many times before.

The two knew each other instantly. Twenty years disappeared. Her beauty, undiminished; his eyes, still pained, still searching.

She was lying on a pallet, her shoulders slightly raised. Her companions had lowered her to the ground and retreated to a respectful distance. They all knew why she was here.

Lorenzo knelt beside her. "Let me help you inside, Beatrice."

She shook her head.

He insisted.

"The monks, Lorenzo, they are afraid. They will not—" she protested.

Lorenzo put his hands under her arms and lifted her tenderly to her feet. With his right arm around her for support, they walked across the stone courtyard and into the church. He had offered to carry her. She had refused.

The light in the lower church was growing dim, but above in the dome the setting sun was still casting its red glow over Lorenzo's paintings. Lorenzo eased Beatrice onto a wooden bench. He asked if she wanted anything. She shook her head. He sat beside her. She looked up.

The church had been dedicated to the Blessed Virgin and there were many scenes with her image. Beatrice looked at each panel, devouring every figure, every saint, every angel.

She turned to Lorenzo. "They are beautiful, Lorenzo. And the Virgin . . ." Beatrice stopped to get her breath. Lorenzo reached out and took her hand in his.

She continued, her voice very weak, "Her face is beautiful, Lorenzo . . . and I see . . . her love . . . for all of us." She looked up at him. Her smile was as warm as he remembered.

Her head rested against his shoulder. He held on to her hand as tightly as he dared without hurting her. He didn't want her to leave. He felt her breathing grow more shallow. He looked at her; she was still looking at the paintings. He had no doubt that many years had passed since she'd seen an image of herself in a mirror, if, indeed, she ever had. She had no idea that the face of the Virgin was her own—the face that Lorenzo had first seen leaning over him surrounded by a crown of golden curls, the face that had implored him to use his gift for good, the face he held so dear that he had given his life and his art to its memory.

The sun set. The shadows in the church deepened. The thin hand in his grew cold. Lorenzo closed his eyes. He saw only the vision of Beatrice and the brief, but timeless moment in that distant summer when his life was changed forever.

AUTHOR'S NOTE

Northern Italy in the fourteenth and fifteenth centuries was divided into city-states. Florence and Milan were two of the most famous independent cities, but there were many more, all competing for power and wealth in a period of history we call the Renaissance. It was a time of unprecedented artistic creativity, expanding commerce, and political turmoil.

In their quest for political advantage, city-states sought alliances with their neighbors. But allies were often unreliable and sometimes treacherous, and war, or the threat of war, was ever present. This led to an arms race; rulers hired famous artists and inventors (such as Leonardo da Vinci) to design fortifications and machines of war. And armies sought the latest in weapons and armor from armorers such as the house of Missaglia in Milan. These armories (like the house of Arrighi in our story) were usually family run and handed down from one generation to the next.

Cities also needed soldiers. Often they hired mercenaries—foreign soldiers—many of whom came from Germany, England, and Spain. Their loyalty, however, was suspect, and some city-states disdained them, preferring to use their own citizen soldiers. This solution worked best when the city-state was led by a ruler who inspired loyalty and respect among his subjects.

One such ruler was Federigo da Montefeltro, duke of Urbino, a great leader both militarily and culturally. His fame as a warrior and the stories explaining the shape of his nose (as seen in a painting by Piero della Francesca) were the inspiration for the duke in our story. The paintings that covered the walls of the duke's chamber were suggested by a series of murals by Andrea Mantegna in the city-state of Mantua.

ABOUT THE ART

The illustrations in *The Warhorse* were designed to resemble excerpts from a Renaissance artist's sketchbook. The drawings were made with colored pencil, and the effects are similar to those in sketches from that period. Renaissance artists often added highlights and details to drawings with touches of white paint, as in the picture of signor Arrighi wearing ceremonial shoulder armor.

Some of the characters in the sketches were influenced by actual drawings and paintings from the Renaissance period. For example, the picture of Beatrice was copied from Leonardo da Vinci's portrait of Ginevra de' Benci (in the National Gallery of Art in Washington, D.C.), and the duke was inspired by Piero della Francesca's painting of Federico da Montefeltro, duke of Urbino (in the Uffizi Gallery in Florence, Italy).

A sketchbook can be a valuable and useful tool—it records the artist's thoughts and design ideas, and functions as a sort of camera, capturing everything of interest to the artist. Sketchbooks can also become records of the artistic and creative thinking of a particular period in history; the famous notebooks of Leonardo da Vinci are a perfect example. The illustrations in this book are intended to capture a sense of Lorenzo's time and place.

ABOUT THE AUTHOR

Don Bolognese was born in New York City to immigrant parents and grew up in an atmosphere of art and Italian culture. A graduate of the Cooper Union School of Art, he determined early on that he would be an illustrator, and after illustrating works by many other authors he decided to write his own books. Among them are several series combining art, history, and adventure, many of which were done in collaboration with his wife, Elaine Raphael, an author and artist.

Several years ago he teamed up with Ms. Raphael to design and illustrate *Letters to Horseface,* the story of Mozart's travels through Italy, by F. N. Monjo. Retracing the young composer's footsteps gave him a firsthand look at the birthplace of the Renaissance. That experience provided the inspiration for *The Warhorse.*

In his spare time Don Bolognese is an avid gardener and a cautious collector of wild mushrooms.